Warwickshire County Council

LEA new 8/19			

This item is to be returned or renewed before the
latest date above. It may be borrowed for a further
period if not in demand. **To renew your books:**

- **Phone the 24/7 Renewal Line 01926 49927**
- **Visit www.warwickshire.gov.uk**

    Discover ● Imagine● Learn

Warwickshire
County Council

Working for Warwickshire

Silent Witness

When Range Detective Rance Dehner stops to make camp he hears a strange sound coming from the surrounding brush. A young girl of about five is hiding there. Her eyes reflect terror and she is unable to speak. Within minutes, someone tries to ambush both Dehner and the child.

Bullets continue to fly as Dehner discovers that the girl witnessed her parents' murder and the horrifying experience has traumatized the child into silence. The detective's investigation leads him into a bizarre small town race for mayor and a whirlpool of violence related to the brutal killing of the girl's parents. Can Dehner discover the shocking truth behind the murders before a town destroys itself?

Silent Witness

James Clay

A Black Horse Western

ROBERT HALE

© James Clay 2019
First published in Great Britain 2019

ISBN 978-0-7198-2967-3

The Crowood Press
The Stable Block
Crowood Lane
Ramsbury
Marlborough
Wiltshire SN8 2HR

www.bhwesterns.com

Robert Hale is an imprint
of The Crowood Press

Typeset by
Derek Doyle & Associates, Shaw Heath
Printed and bound in Great Britain by
4Bind Ltd, Stevenage, SG1 2XT

CHAPTER ONE

Waves of relentless heat passed in front of Rance Dehner as he rode further and further away from what had been a bloody confrontation in an Arizona town. Three days back Dehner had killed two men: men who needed killing. He had retrieved the money they had stolen from a bank. But two of the outlaws had gotten away and Dehner's assignment remained uncompleted: kill or capture all members of a gang that had been terrorizing the area.

The detective gazed at the purple mountains which stood like a stone fortress. Their strength and timelessness seemed to mock him. Rance felt weary and wondered if his life was becoming a strange sort of trap. Could he ever settle down and start a ranch or open a store or do any of the things normal men do to make a living?

The question made him restless. Noon was still an hour or more away but a belt of water looped down nearby from the mountains. He decided to make camp, fix some food and take time to read. Two books were in his saddlebags: a Bible and a volume containing *Hamlet* and *King Lear*.

Dehner planned to opt for Shakespeare. He was in a mood for tragedy.

Without prompting, his horse began to move faster as they approached the water. The detective halted near a large grove of trees. He dismounted, allowed his horse to drink, then bent down and began to cup water in his hands.

A cracking noise sounded from the trees. Instinctively, Dehner sprang to his feet and drew his .45. The sound continued but Dehner couldn't place it. Whatever was behind those trees didn't sound like an animal or a man, at least not a man who was trying to keep his presence a secret.

The sound was coming closer. Dehner watched intently as a few branches parted and a child stepped out.

The detective holstered his weapon and smiled at the girl as he slowly approached her. Dehner figured the kid to be about five years of age. She had blondish-brown hair, a round face and blue eyes that were vacant. Rance smiled as he crouched in front of the child.

'Hello.'

The girl said nothing. Her eyes looked directly at Dehner, but her expression conveyed no emotion. Her dress was tattered and her shoes covered with dirt.

'My name is Rance. What's your name?'

The girl remained silent.

'Do you know where your mommy or daddy are?'

The child said nothing and Dehner stopped with the questions. The look on the girl's face caused him to pause. He had seen that empty expression before, on the faces of people who had witnessed death and destruction on a massive scale.

The detective sighed inwardly. He had been through hell three days ago. He had a feeling this little girl had been through something even worse. Dehner tried to keep his voice friendly and kind.

'For a little while, I'm going to call you Pixie. A pixie is sort of like an elf. Some folks say pixies live in the woods.' He nodded with his head toward the grove of trees the girl had just emerged from. 'You can be Pixie for a while, then you can get your real name back.'

The girl didn't respond. Dehner didn't really expect her

to. He knew the area reasonably well. Candler was the nearest town. If he couldn't find the kid's home or her family he would take her there.

'Come take a ride on my horse.' Dehner kept his voice happy and upbeat, though he suspected the girl didn't really care. 'Maybe we can find your people.'

Pixie didn't resist as Rance lifted the child up, carried her to his horse and seated her on the saddle. He then climbed up behind her and carefully looked over the rocky area. The stream got larger as it flowed east from the mountains and the land became greener. A good place for a ranch; maybe he could find some people there who would recognize Pixie.

The detective kept an eye on the girl as they rode in the direction of green land. He paid no heed to the row of boulders on their left side.

Dehner's horse went up on two legs as the sound of a shot echoed off the mountains. Pixie screamed and jumped from the bay, landing on her face. She scrambled up and began to run back toward the grove of trees. The sound of a second shot whined over the land.

Dehner drew his Colt and fired twice toward the boulders. The move was primarily intended to provide cover as he grabbed a Winchester from its boot. He slid off the bay and ran toward the girl, snapping off a shot at the attacker with his .45 while toting the Winchester in his left hand.

He caught up with Pixie and pushed her to the ground. The girl continued to scream hysterically.

'Stay down!' Dehner yelled as he crouched on one knee in front of the child. He hastily dropped his Colt and aimed the Winchester toward the boulders.

He saw sunlight glint off the barrel of a rifle and sent a red spear in that direction. A man's yell echoed across the mountain range, mixing with the sounds of a ricocheting bullet. Dehner reckoned his shot had missed the mark but the enemy had been injured or somehow scared off in his attempt to duck.

There came sounds of a horse or horses in retreat. Dehner couldn't tell if there was more than one horse: Pixie's crying overwhelmed the hoofbeats.

Rance lifted the child to her feet and spoke calming words as he put his arms around her. It didn't work. The detective had to give Pixie about ten minutes to exhaust herself with the loud cries. As she screamed Dehner tried to get her to talk, to tell him at least a little bit about what had happened to her. That didn't work either. Finally he was able to take the girl by the hand and walk with her back to his horse. The bay gelding was now grazing on some grass that lined the stream.

Pixie had again become silent. Rance found that to be more nerve-racking than the screams. He decided not to try and locate Pixie's family. He needed to get the child into town and make sure she was safe.

And he needed to find out who was trying to kill her.

CHAPTER TWO

Dehner rode slowly into the town of Candler. He had known of the town's existence but never been there. Rance was a stranger. He hoped Pixie wasn't.

His eyes gazed through the large open doorway of Brighton's Mercantile. A man wearing a badge stood inside talking with a couple behind the counter. All three of them gave the stranger arriving in town a curious look.

The detective pegged Brighton's Mercantile as a good place to start. He dismounted and lifted Pixie down. The child remained in an almost trancelike state. Dehner couldn't tell if Pixie recognized the town or not. He tied up his horse, took the little girl's hand, and walked with her into the store.

There were smiles all around, though the smile from the middle-aged man with a piece of bright tin hanging on his shirt was tentative. The local law often greeted Dehner with caution. *Even having a cute little kid with you doesn't change that*, the detective mused.

'Howdy. The name is Clint Mead, I'm the sheriff around here.' Clint Mead was a big-shouldered man with a wide, craggy face. Dust covered his pants but his shirt and the badge on it were clean. Rance wondered if changing his shirt regularly was the sheriff's concession to mannerly behavior. The sheriff nodded at his two companions.

'This here is Enoch Brighton, the owner of this establishment. The pretty little filly standing next to him is Sylvia Kaplan. She keeps Enoch on his toes.'

Enoch was tall, barrel-chested, with thick black sideburns that connected with a small neatly trimmed beard. He appeared to be in his mid-twenties. His arms were huge, more the arms of a lumberjack than a storekeeper. Sylvia was a few years younger. She was indeed pretty, though her lips had pressed together when the sheriff described her. She had auburn hair, green eyes and a mischievous smile which gave her a slightly tomboyish appearance.

'The name is Rance Dehner.' The detective didn't mention his primary reason for being in town. That could come later.

'You must be friends with the Scotts,' Enoch said.

Dehner shook his head. Enoch looked confused as he pointed at Rance's companion.

'That little girl is Jenny Scott; she's the daughter of Josh and Tillie Scott.'

Dehner glanced at Jenny. To his disappointment she gave no reaction to hearing her name, the name of her parents, or to seeing people she knew.

The detective gave a brief account of how he had found Jenny, including the fact that someone was trying to kill the child. He explained that he was a detective with the Lowrie Agency.

Sylvia Kaplan gently asked Jenny about what had happened that morning and received the same silent response Rance had received earlier. Finally, the young woman looked down and shook her head in worried defeat. Rance intruded on her mood with a question.

'Are the Scotts regular customers here?'

Sylvia nodded her head. 'Like a lot of folks, they come into town every Saturday to do their shopping and some socializing.'

'Last Saturday . . .' the detective briefly paused to reflect on the fact that it was Thursday, 'that was five days ago; were they here then?'

Enoch and Sylvia exchanged glances and said 'Yes', almost in unison. Dehner responded with another question.

'Did they act in a . . . well . . . strange manner? Did they say anything that might indicate they were expecting trouble?'

The store-owner shrugged his shoulders. 'Nope.'

'But Tillie and Jenny didn't stay all that long,' Sylvia added. 'As I recall, we were out of candy – we have trouble keeping it in stock. So Tillie took Jenny to the store across the street. She may have said something there. . . .'

'I don't like the sound of this,' the sheriff interjected. 'Think I'd better ride out to the Scott ranch.' He stared at Jenny for a moment. 'I got a feelin' it might be too late.'

'Where is the ranch located?' Dehner asked.

'A few miles from here, where the creek begins to turn into a river,' the lawman answered.

'Exactly where I found Pix – Jenny,' Rance said. 'Do you mind if I ride along with you?'

'Well no, but. . . .' The lawman looked toward Jenny.

Dehner suddenly realized that he was sort of responsible for the child.

'Maybe—'

'I'll look after Jenny,' Sylvia cut in, 'until . . . until her people are found.'

Rance looked uncertain and the young woman sensed what he was thinking.

'Mr Dehner, my father taught me to hunt. There's a shotgun under this counter and a Henry at home where I live with my mother. Jenny will be safe as long as she is with me.'

'You can bet on it, Rance!' Enoch bellowed. 'Not only can Sylvia hunt good, she can sure cook those varmints she shoots – real fine.'

Sylvia looked pleased by the compliment. 'Mr Brighton,

would it be OK if I took Jenny home for a spell? She needs some cleaning up and maybe some food.'

Enoch crunched up his face. 'Could ya jus' keep her here for a few hours? I got some things that need doin'. After that, if need be, ya can take her home and take the rest of the day off.'

'Thank you, Mr Brighton. If Jenny's people can't be found right off. . . ?'

'Ya can bring Jenny with ya to the store. Give her one of them rag dolls we sell, it'll keep her busy. I'll pay for it.'

A broad smile covered the young woman's face and Dehner speculated on the couple's interaction. Sylvia had been confident and assertive when assuring Rance she could take care of Jenny. But that confidence had weakened when she asked a favor of her boss. And Enoch had seemed to enjoy being generous to his employee.

'I gotta find that new deputy of mine and fill him in on some things he's gotta do while I'm gone.' Sheriff Mead's voice cut in on Dehner's private thoughts. 'My office is right up the street. Could ya meet me there in 'bout twenty minutes?'

'Sure,' Dehner responded. 'I'll use the time to talk to the folks in the store across the street. Maybe Tillie Scott said something that could help us.'

But as Rance left the store Clint Mead's words echoed in his mind: *I got a feelin' it might be too late.*

CHAPTER THREE

The Bushrod brothers' general store was located across the street from Brighton's Mercantile but seemed to exist in a different world. The place looked dilapidated. Even from a distance Dehner could tell that the inside of the store would have a look of disrepair and negligence.

As he stepped inside he noted that the store had one customer, a dapper-looking older man in a tan suit and matching derby. On second glance, Dehner wasn't sure the gentleman was a customer. His face indicated that, whatever his status, he was not happy. As the well-dressed gent turned to walk out a stocky man with thick red hair grabbed a stick of licorice from a large jar on the counter and ran after him.

'Here, Mr Candler, have some licorice on the house. Remember when you was just a boy and somethin' sweet to eat would make everythin' better?'

Judging by the scowl on his face Mr Candler did not appreciate the reminiscing.

'When I became a man I put away childish things,' he proclaimed. The man holding the licorice stick beamed in an approving manner.

'Good thinkin', Mr Candler. This town needs more men like you. Men who are well-versed in the Good Book! I'll tell that to the preacher . . . ah . . . next time I see him.'

Mr Candler stomped out of the Bushrod brothers' general

store. The red-headed gent with the licorice stick shook his head.

'The way that man acts, you'd think his family owns the town.'

'They do,' came a shout from behind the counter. 'This is Candler, Arizona, remember?'

'Oh, I keep forgettin' that.' The red-headed man took a bite of the licorice stick and smiled at Dehner.

There were quick introductions all around. Rance learned that the man with the licorice was Rupert Bushrod, and the man behind the counter was his brother Clarence. The men were twins, and could easily have passed for each other except for Clarence's thicker waistline.

'Sorry you had to arrive when we were so busy, Rance.' Rupert leaned against the counter as he took a final bite of the candy. 'Mr Candler is the town banker. He's a mite irritated with Clarence and me . . . or is that Clarence and I? . . . because we ain't made our payments of late.'

'It's "Clarence and me",' Dehner instructed, then asked: 'You mean you haven't been able to make your mortgage payments?'

Clarence shrugged his shoulders. 'Right now there are so many payments we are behind on; you can pretty much take your pick. We got lots of payments, not many customers. Most folks prefer to shop at Brighton's Mercantile. Can't figure out why.'

Rupert held up an index finger. 'Maybe it's 'cause Enoch Brighton and Sylvia Kaplan are more helpful, their store is cleaner and their prices lower.'

Clarence nodded his head in a thoughtful manner. 'Guess that could have somethin' to do with it.'

'Maybe you can help us out, Rance?' Hope permeated Rupert's voice. 'We got anythin' here you'd like to buy?'

'I was hoping you gents could help me. I understand Tillie Scott was in your store last Saturday. Do you remember. . . ?'

'Oh yes.' Clarence's voice was a near shout. 'I remember ever' time Tillie has entered these unworthy premises. Tillie is a really beautiful woman. She brought the kid here because they was sold out of candy across the street.'

'We never sell out of nothin',' Rupert added.

'How long did Tillie stay in your store?' Dehner threw the question out to either brother. Rupert caught it.

'Not long enough. Did we mention that she was real good lookin'?'

'I recall words to that effect,' the detective said. 'Did the lady say anything about problems she and her husband were having . . . like someone threatening them?'

'Nah,' Rupert said. 'After she bought the kid some gum-drops she talked for a few minutes 'bout the horse ranch she and Josh run. Then she looked out the door and saw Enoch helpin' her husband load up his buckboard. She took the girl and went to lend a hand.'

'Is that the last time you saw her?'

' 'Fraid so.' Clarence ran a hand through his hair. 'Seems a shame, a beautiful woman like that workin' out on a ranch when she could have a great job right here in town as a saloon girl.'

'The kid did come back for a minute,' Rupert added. 'She brought a penny with her and bought some more candy.'

'It's gettin' to the point where we remember every sale we make with great fondness,' Clarence declared.

'Thanks for the information, gentlemen.' Dehner placed a couple of coins on the counter and took several pieces of gumdrops from a jar. He returned to Brighton's Mercantile and gave them to Sylvia. 'Jenny might enjoy a little something sweet.'

As he left Sylvia was trying to hand the candy to Jenny. The child continued to stare straight ahead, not really seeing Sylvia or the gumdrops. Dehner wondered what terrible visions filled the child's mind.

CHAPTER FOUR

As Rance entered the sheriff's office Clint Mead was talking to a nervous young man who kept working his hands and nodding his head. The tin on the jittery man's shirt was shiny and looked like he had polished it that morning.

'One more thing,' Clint seemed to be coming to the end of a long list. 'His honour the mayor will expect ya to meet the stage when it comes in. If you spot any jasper that looks like trouble, talk to him. If he ain't gotta good reason for bein' in town, tell him to jus' stay on the stage. Ya've seen me do it a few times.'

'Yes, Sheriff, I can handle it.'

Mead gave the detective a quick glance. 'Ah, Deputy Boone Logan, this here is Rance. . . .'

'Dehner.' Rance shook the hand of a man who was probably in his early twenties. His long oval face was topped by sand-colored hair ending in a curl that bobbed over his forehead.

'We gotta be leavin',' the sheriff said. 'Try to see that the town is still here when we get back, Deputy.'

'Yes, Sheriff.' Boone's voice sounded contrite.

Detective instincts were not required to notice that Clint Mead was not happy with his new deputy. Rance waited until he and the sheriff had ridden out of Candler before asking: 'Boone Logan not working out too well?'

16

Mead began to talk in the fast, jerky manner of a man getting something off his chest. 'Boone is a good kid, but he's got trouble acceptin' the way we do things in this town. Guess I can't blame him . . . ain't his fault. Bernard Candler is a strange old bird and he makes for a crazy mayor.'

The mayor's last name sparked recognition in Dehner. 'Bernard Candler: is that the same gent who's the town banker?'

'The same. He's done some good for this town – ain't sayin' different, but times are changin' and Bernie ain't.'

Dehner gave the sheriff a sardonic smile. 'Meeting the stage and telling people who look suspicious to stay on it – well, in a way that might be a good idea but it's illegal.'

'I know. Boone's already gettin' hisself into a lather 'bout it all. But his honour wants Candler to be a quiet, peaceful town. He makes us keep an eye on ever' newcomer. If a jasper ain't got a job in a week, we gotta run him out. Why, Bernie's even fightin' against the railroad comin' into Candler.'

'Why?' Dehner asked. 'The railroad would bring a lot of prosperity to the town.'

'Yep, but it would also bring a lot more people and a lot of hoorawin' that Bernie couldn't control. Candler wouldn't be so quiet or peaceful no more.'

Dehner continued to eye the terrain as he thought over what the lawman had just told him. The Lowrie Agency had done some work for several railroads and Rance was well aware of the operations of that powerful industry: the good and the bad.

'What do the fine citizens of Candler think about the mayor's notions?' he asked.

'We're 'bout to find out.'

'What do you mean?'

'For as long as anyone can remember Bernard Candler has run for mayor with nobody opposin' him.'

17

Dehner saw where this was leading. 'But that is about to change?'

'Yep.' Clint laughed caustically. 'That's what I was in Brighton's Mercantile talkin' 'bout when you rode in with Jenny. Enoch Brighton is runnin' against Bernie Candler for mayor. Enoch registered today. The election is comin' up a week from this Saturday.'

'Are you supporting Enoch?'

'Sure am. Now, Enoch can't promise he'll get the railroad into Candler but he's willin' enough to try. Enoch is a young fella with a lot of sand. Bernard can run his bank for as long as he likes but I don't think he'll be runnin' the town much longer.'

Dehner suddenly pulled up and pointed to his right.

'That's the grove of trees where I found Jenny . . . or she found me.' He shifted his arm in order to point forward. 'I was carrying Jenny in that direction when we were ambushed.'

Mead nodded his head. 'Ya was probably takin' the kid home, even though you didn't know it at the time. The Scotts have their ranch up ahead.'

Then both men suddenly went silent, stunned by what they saw.

'Looks like smoke,' Rance said.

'Yep. Right where the Scotts' ranch is. . . .'

Dehner and the sheriff spurred their horses into a fast gallop. The ears of Dehner's bay went back and his mane began a wild dance. Landscape whizzed by. As their horses ate up the ground the men could see a large ranch house being consumed by fire.

Dehner focused on the horror in front of him, and the detective repeated a mistake he had made only hours before. He ignored the large rocks surrounding the mountain to his left. Once again, the mistake was dangerous.

The pop of rifle shots mingled with the crackling sounds

of fire. The two riders reined off toward a large barn that stood about twenty yards away from the burning house. They dismounted, pulled rifles from their saddle boots and let both horses run.

'They'll head for water,' the sheriff yelled. 'We'll find 'em.'

The double doors of the barn were open; both men ran inside and looked toward the boulders fronting the mountain.

'Any idea of how many of 'em there are – or where they are?' Mead asked as his eyes searched the rocky area.

'No. And we've got no time to think about it. Cover me, I'm going inside the house.'

'Are you sure there's people in there?'

'Probably are. And they may be alive. Why else would someone be firing at us?'

Clint nodded his head as the detective dropped his rifle, crouched into a jackknife position and ran toward the house. Gunfire ignited again. One shot shattered a front window of the house. Dehner kept moving toward the angry clouds of smoke that flowed from an open front door.

Dehner held his breath and plowed through the gray billows to be confronted by a red death which was gorging on the back wall of the house and spreading fast to the ceiling. Suddenly, the fire seemed to be coming at him like a wild animal that had just picked up the scent of a new victim.

Two bodies lay on the floor, a man and a woman. Dehner lifted the woman's body, placed her over his shoulder and ran back to the doorway. The need to breathe became intense as he charged into the streaming smoke.

Gunshots greeted him as he ran off the porch and onto the yard of the ranch house, pulling in deep lungfuls of the outside air. Dehner hastily placed the body down, then dropped to the ground himself. From the corner of his eye he could see an explosive flash, which cut the air like a monstrous lightning bolt. A massive fireworks display of red then

19

covered the sky as the roof of the house collapsed.

The detective glanced backward at the rampaging fire. The man he had left in the house was beyond rescue.

The flames continued their destructive rampage. The roof of the barn was now on fire. Dehner wondered how long Clint Mead could remain safely inside.

As if answering the question, Mead ran from the barn to where he could stand beside the detective. No shots came from the mountain area.

'I think they've gone, Rance,' Clint shouted. 'I heard hoofbeats when the house came down. Can't say how many there was.'

Dehner sprang to his feet. No one fired, but the beast behind him seemed to be growing. He picked up the body of the young woman and carried her a safe distance from the smoke and flames.

'Is she still alive, Rance?'

'Don't know.' Dehner coughed as he gently placed the woman on the ground.

'You OK?' the sheriff asked.

'I'm fine.' Both men crouched over the body.

'This is the Scott woman,' the sheriff said.

Dehner coughed once again, his eyes were still watering from the smoke.

'She was shot at close range,' he said. 'Someone killed her and then set fire to the house.'

'Why would they do that?'

'Don't know. Her husband was probably shot, too.' Dehner glanced back at the inferno, which now raged where a house had been. 'It'll be a while before we can retrieve his body.'

Dehner turned back and looked at Tillie Scott's body.

'Have you seen many corpses, Clint?'

'Yes.'

'Me too. I don't think this woman was killed recently. She's been dead at least a few hours.'

The sheriff took a closer look at the dead body. He was holding two rifles: his own and Rance's.

'You're right. That means the Scotts were probably killed this mornin'.'

'Yes, about the time I met up with Jenny.'

'But why would the killers come back and set fire to the house?'

Dehner shook his head. 'I can't say. All we know for sure is that someone murdered the parents of a little girl. And now they want to kill the child.'

CHAPTER FIVE

'So, Rance, ya plan on staying in Candler for a while?' Deputy Boone Logan's voice was cheerful as he handed Dehner a tin cup of coffee.

Dehner nodded his thanks. 'Yes.'

'Why's that?' Clint Mead asked.

The three men were gathered in the sheriff's office. Clint and Rance had just returned from taking the corpse of Tillie Scott to the undertaker.

'The Lowrie Agency has been hired by Wells Fargo to stop a gang of killers that have reaped a lot of destruction in this area: killing, robbing banks – and, of course, pulling stage-coach hold-ups, which is what interests Wells Fargo.'

'From what ya say, sounds like you're doing a good job already.' Boone's voice was still cheerful. 'Ya killed two members of the gang.'

'I'm not sure that really accomplished much,' Dehner replied.

'I don't follow you.' Sheriff Mead was sitting behind the one desk in the office. The other two men were walking about restlessly while avoiding a collision with the stove which stood topped by a coffee pot and was the only other item on the office's rough wooden floor.

'I was working with a US marshal named Mark Reno when we caught up with the gang. They had just robbed a small-town bank. I managed to bring down two of them but the other two got away. The marshal recognized the two dead men. He told me they were low-level crooks. We parted company after that. Reno is working on a case involving gun-running into Mexico.'

'Which one of them sides are they sellin' the guns to?' Boone asked.

'The one with the most money,' Dehner answered.

'Figures.' The deputy laughed.

'The marshal is a good man,' Clint declared. 'He was in town a few months back, seein' if he could find anything on the gun-smugglers. I gave him all the help I could, which wasn't much. We studied some maps and I came up with the notion that the gang is operatin' out of Yuma. I think he's lookin' into that now.'

Dehner smiled approvingly. 'Sounds to me like you were more help to Marshal Reno than you give yourself credit for.'

Sheriff Mead wanted to get back to the subject at hand. 'The two men who got away, when ya stopped the bank hold-up, ya trailed 'em here?'

'They seemed headed for Candler.' Dehner paused and took a sip of his coffee. His eyebrows immediately shot up. Clint gave the detective a lopsided smile.

'Boone's coffee takes some gettin' used to.'

The deputy's response was quick and defensive. 'But it sure does carry a punch, don't ya think?'

'That it does.' Dehner took a second, more cautious sip, then continued: 'We know how most gangs operate. They pull a job, split up the loot, and after that, go their separate ways for a while.'

'They usually make plans to meet up somewhere in a few months.'

Sheriff Mead began to pack tobacco into a pipe as he spoke. 'By that time, the leader's got another job all planned out.'

'I'm not sure that's the case here,' Dehner said.

Clint struck a match against his desk. 'Why not?'

The detective replied slowly as if trying to bring his own ideas into clear focus.

'For a gang that's been pulling jobs for over a year, that bunch I encountered a few days ago didn't seem to work together very well, not all four of them anyway.'

Mead ignited his pipe. 'What are ya gettin' at, Rance?'

'I think maybe this gang has only two members who are both smart and vicious. They hire on a couple of thugs to help them with each job. Once the job is done, they kill the extra help. Last Saturday I did their dirty work for them.'

'You're talkin' 'bout two greedy crooks who don't want to split the money from a job,' Boone said. Clint removed the pipe from his mouth and pointed it at Rance.

'Do you think these two owlhoots are using Candler as a base?'

'It does make sense,' the detective answered. 'They could be posing as respectable citizens. And the murder of Josh and Tillie Scott could be connected somehow. Those killings were so strange. Not many killers are animal lovers.'

'Whadda ya mean?' Boone looked confused.

'The Scotts raised horses,' Rance answered. 'But there were no horses in the barn or in the corral behind the barn. The barn doors stood open. The corral was on fire by the time I spotted it but there were no horses in that corral and I'd bet that the gate had also been opened.'

'Maybe the killers were horse thieves,' the sheriff suggested from behind a thin screen of smoke. 'Or maybe they wanted us to think they were horse thieves and just turned the animals loose.'

Dehner paused to slosh his coffee about in the cup. 'I can't help but think that Jenny is somehow involved in all of this. She witnessed something terrible, something which could be connected with the killers we're after.'

'Ya may be right,' Boone shrugged his shoulders, 'but what good does it do if ya can't get the girl to speak?'

No one in the room could answer the question.

CHAPTER SIX

Sylvia Kaplan stood on the porch of her small home, talking with two men who had called on her that evening. They were conversing in low voices. Jenny was in the living room of the house and Sylvia's mother was trying to read to her.

'I can't find anything physically wrong with the child.' The words came from Doctor Reginald Dalrymple, a large, ruggedly built man of about fifty, with a face dominated by a large forehead that seemed to create caverns for his two dark eyes. His cheeks were hollow. Most folks in Candler knew that the doctor didn't get much sleep but that didn't affect his disposition, which was usually amicable. Doctor Dalrymple enjoyed the nickname 'Doc Reggie' by which he was known.

'When will she start talking again?' Sylvia asked.

'I don't know,' the doctor replied. Sylvia shook her head in frustration.

'Isn't there anything we can do?'

'Maybe,' Reggie replied in a slow, cautious manner, 'but I don't want to discuss it right now ... I need to give the matter serious thought.' He smiled in the direction of the man who was standing on the other side of Sylvia. 'And of course, I need to give it serious prayer.'

Reverend Giles Hobart nervously smiled back. Since he had arrived in town to become pastor of the accurately named First Church of Candler six months before, the preacher had given Sylvia the impression of a man who always seemed to be apologizing for something. Giles had just entered into his thirties. He stood at average height, was thin with dark hair topping a moon-shaped face. He raised an index finger as he spoke.

'A few hours ago I talked with Deputy Boone Logan and that detective . . . ah. . . .'

'Rance Dehner,' Sylvia said.

'Yes, yes.' Giles waved his finger in a thank-you gesture and then continued: 'They told me what happened out at the Scott ranch this afternoon. Terrible! They asked for my help.'

Reverend Hobart paused for a moment, as if basking in the fact that someone had asked for his help. 'We need to make sure this house is safe at all times. I have contacted the men in our congregation who live in town. I have made up a schedule for the week. There will be someone on guard throughout the night, every night. The first sentry will be arriving within the hour.'

'That's wonderful – thank you so much, Pastor.' Sylvia smiled at Reverend Hobart. She felt genuinely happy for him. The pastor seemed so glad to be doing something practical and helpful. Maybe all these terrible events would help him connect with the people of Candler. After six months he still seemed to be an outsider.

There were polite goodbyes and then both men departed. As he headed for his home, which was also his office, Doc Reggie looked with sympathy at Reverend Hobart. The pastor was walking toward the church where he also had an office-home. Reginald spoke out loud to himself. 'That poor man is desperately lonely and desperately in love with Sylvia Kaplan, who is in love with her boss.'

The doctor smiled in a whimsical manner as he reflected on his marriage of twenty-five years, which had produced two sons, both of whom were now practicing medicine in St

Louis. Though now a widower, thoughts of Madelynn always made him smile.

He stepped onto the porch of his house and began to pet the gigantic beast that greeted him. The mongrel dog had short brown hair, sharp teeth and a huge tongue which he was now applying to Reggie's face.

'I've been very blessed, Goliath,' he told the dog. 'I hope Reverend Hobart has the same good fortune.' Goliath responded with two loud barks as Doc Reggie continued to talk to him: 'But something is bothering our preacher friend – bothering him a lot.'

Giles Hobart slowly walked down the middle aisle of his church. There were ten pews on each side of him. The pastor reflected on the first time he had walked into the sanctuary. His heart had been filled with excitement and joy. After serving as an associate pastor at a large church in Denver, he now had his own ministry, an opportunity to. . . ?

The pastor collapsed onto a front pew and bowed his head but not in prayer. That first Sunday in Candler came back to him vividly as did those words of scripture that seemed constantly to haunt him: . . . *be sure your sins will find you out.*

He had spotted her in the congregation early in the service. As he walked to the pulpit to deliver his first sermon he had seen the impish smile on her face. Had she been encouraging him – or mocking him?

Tillie was not alone. She was sitting with a man and a little girl. After the service she gave no sign that she recognized him and perhaps he read too much into her words:

'Welcome to Candler, Pastor, I hope everything will go well for you here.'

Tillie had returned for the evening service but this time she was alone. Before the service began he had heard her talking to Sheriff Mead:

28

'Jenny has a slight fever, Josh is staying home with her. Too bad, because both of them enjoy church, though I suspect Josh would never admit it.'

After the evening service Tillie had said nothing to the pastor as the congregation streamed outside. Once everyone was gone, he had wandered about the sanctuary, tidying up and wrestling with his own thoughts.

'Hello, Giles.'

How had she re-entered the church without making any noise? Those wooden double doors were heavy and. . . .

Tillie had walked ghostlike out of the darkness of the church's front lobby into the sanctuary where the kerosene lights fastened on the side walls seemed to spotlight her. She was more beautiful than ever.

'Tillie, I . . . it's good to see you again.'

Once again, there was that impish smile. 'I think you really mean it.'

'You must know how—'

'We've no time for small talk, Giles. My buggy is out front and it can't stay there long without setting off gossipy tongues.'

'Yes, yes, of course.'

'I am now Mrs Joshua Scott. Jenny, who you saw this morning, is our daughter.' She saw the confusion on his face and responded to it. 'Jenny was born to a friend of mine in Denver. That friend is dead now and I'm raising Jenny. She and Joshua are the most important things in my life. Don't you forget that, Giles.'

'I won't. Tell me, do you—'

'Yes,' Tillie cut in. 'I still practice some of my old habits. But don't worry – I also practice the same caution. Both of us are safe. From now on you will call me Mrs Scott and I will address you as Reverend Hobart. Good evening, Reverend.'

She began to walk towards the double doors. The woman suddenly stopped, turned and faced the pastor. 'You were always a sweet man.'

'Thank you, I try—'

'But like a lot of sweet men you were also weak,' Tillie's voice was accusatory. 'Be careful, Reverend Hobart. If you do anything to harm my husband or child, I'll kill you.' She vanished into the darkness.

Giles Hobart lifted himself from the front pew and gazed over the sanctuary. It looked almost exactly as it had on that strange night. But Tillie would never walk down that center aisle again.

. . . be sure your sins will find you out.

He couldn't allow that to happen. Tomorrow, people would be riding out to the Scott ranch to retrieve the body of Joshua Scott. He couldn't take any chances. Giles left the church through the front doors and moved with haste to the small stable behind the building. He saddled his horse and quietly rode a back path out of town.

CHAPTER SEVEN

Giles pulled up his horse and stared at the carnage before him.

'Hell is spilling over,' he whispered to himself.

What had been the Scotts' ranch was now no more than a pile of rubble, with red cinders glowing like loose particles from Hades. Smoke was still rising up from the ruins.

Reverend Hobart wanted to turn his buckskin and ride back into town. After all, what were the chances that anyone would find. . . ?

The pastor closed his eyes, inhaled and tried to steady himself. After tonight, it would all be over with: one grisly task and he'd be safe.

He guided his horse to the boulders that faced what had been the Scott ranch. He tethered the buckskin to the ground behind the largest boulder. The horse wasn't completely covered but anyone riding by that late at night and pausing to look at the wreckage would be unlikely to spot the animal. He put on a pair of gloves from the saddle-bags and freed a lantern he had tied to the saddle.

Hobart placed the lantern on the ground and took a box of matches from his pocket. He took a match from the box, put a flame to the lantern and watched the glow increase.

As the pastor picked up the lantern an odd desire overwhelmed him. He wanted to pray, to ask the Lord to bring him success in his mission.

That would be an act of blasphemy, he said to himself as he began to walk toward the wreckage. *Later I will pray . . . pray for forgiveness.*

As Hobart drew near to the ruins a horrible stench enveloped him. Men who had experienced the horrors of burnt flesh had told him of that awful smell, but he was still unprepared for it. The pastor stopped for a moment, then continued his journey, then stopped again. He hastily put the light down and vomited.

As he picked up the lantern the pastor spotted several coyotes watching him with intense curiosity. The animals had been attracted by the smell but the smoke and heat still coming from the ruination kept them back; animals who survived in the wild developed instincts about fire.

Giles Hobart began a laugh which morphed into a cry. He was going into a wretched arena that was shunned by the most loathsome of beasts. Then, once again, Hobart paused and tried to compose himself. He had come this far. He could go further.

The pastor raised the lantern and slowly moved the light over the destruction. Where to even begin?

Hope suddenly gripped him. There, near the far left corner of the destruction: was that what it appeared to be? Hobart's steps created clouds of ashes as he moved toward the object. Yes, it was the base of a bedpost.

Giles tossed a few burnt boards to the side to allow space for the lantern. He then began to clear the rubble with his hands until he came to a braided rag rug. The rug had been badly singed but was still in one piece. He'd be willing to bet there were a few other such rugs in this area which must have been the bedroom. Two or three rag rugs in the room would not call attention to any one of the rugs.

He crouched over the rug and gently tugged it. The rug was nailed to the floor. Tillie had told him the truth. She practiced her old habits and with the same caution.

Hobart picked up the lantern and moved it over the rug until he spotted the nail heads. The rug had been nailed down, but in a loose manner, so that it could be lifted with a minimum of fuss. The only purpose of the nails was to keep the rug in place, where it could camouflage what was underneath.

The pastor pulled a coin from his pocket and employed it to loosen two nails. He then pulled the rug back, revealing a trapdoor. One nail remained in the middle of the rug, holding it to the door. Tillie had kept her secret place at her bedside, just as she had back in the days when. . . .

Reverend Hobart checked his thoughts. This was not a time for reminiscing. He opened the trapdoor, revealing a ladder that had not been touched by the flames. Lantern in hand, Giles made his way down the steps. The pastor tried to ease the trapdoor down but it still made a banging sound as it closed behind him, sending a shock wave through his body. Giles paused on the ladder as his arms and legs trembled. He closed his eyes and tried to quell the panic building inside him. A quick descent into this dark hell would allow him to keep his secret forever.

He moved downwards, stepped off the ladder and moved the lantern about. Tillie had, in all likelihood, prodded her husband to dig this hideaway. There was enough room for three people to hide but not much more. He moved the light along the ground and quickly spotted a large metal case.

'Looks like something a bank would use to keep money or important papers,' Hobart whispered to himself. 'And it's locked . . . God knows where the key to that lock is.'

Reverend Hobart's reference to the Divine caused him once again to tremble. He tried lifting the case but it was too heavy. He couldn't get it up the ladder.

Giles did another fast inspection of the area. There was nothing else there. What he needed had to be in that box, though he had no idea what else Tillie had hidden away that caused the case to be so heavy. The pastor leaned against the ladder and began to weep.

'That's right, cry like a baby, Hobart. Tillie was right, you're weak and. . . .'

An idea came to him. He took two steps away from the ladder, dropped to his knees and began to dig in the dirt with his hands. As gravel flew around him he felt as if his soul was moving backwards into an animal-like primitiveness. Hateful thoughts filled his mind: hate for God, hate for Tillie and, most of all, hate for himself.

When the hole was big enough he placed the metal case in it, covered it with the gravel and packed the dirt in.

'Two steps directly in front of the ladder,' again he whispered to himself. 'I'll come back in a day or two . . . bring a heavy rope; I'll get that case up and out of here.'

Exhausted, the pastor stood up and began to examine himself. His entire body was covered with dirt and ashes. For some reason he began to laugh uncontrollably.

Gunfire sounded from upstairs. Giles Hobart stopped laughing and listened.

'Damn coyotes!' a voice boomed.

Those coyotes must have entered the rubble of the Scott ranch. But why would anyone bother to stop and run them off, especially at this late hour? Unless. . . .

The pastor listened as footsteps sounded from above. He was not the only one with a terrible secret hidden under the ashes and destruction. Someone was obviously carrying out a search.

Panic again gripped Giles Hobart. Whoever it was up there, was he searching for the metal case? Did he know about Tillie's strange notions, and if not, would he still discover the trapdoor?

Crashing sounds of rubble being thrown around blended with the footsteps. Perspiration streamed down Giles's face and his breathing became fast and erratic. The noise sounded closer as the intruder continued to plow his way toward the bedroom.

Suddenly the racket ceased. There was a loud cry of victory. The intruder had found what he was looking for. Giles had not recognized the source of the cry or the voice cursing the coyotes. And he didn't care. He was only concerned with his own treachery not being revealed.

He picked up the lantern, climbed the ladder and paused on the last step. Within a few minutes he heard the sound of hoofbeats. He still waited a while before opening the door and looking outside.

The coyotes were again approaching the ruins but there was no sign of human life. Giles stepped off the ladder, closed the trapdoor, retrieved the nails and returned them to their function of holding the rug in place. He had been wrong. Tonight had not ended his ordeal.

'I'll have to return to this awful place,' he said aloud.

But who was the other man who had been frantically searching above him? Giles realized he wasn't the only individual in Candler carrying a terrible secret.

He returned to his horse, doused the lantern and rode back in darkness.

CHAPTER EIGHT

Bernard Candler's desk was large but not ornamental. The papers on top of it were neatly arranged. Four walls separated Candler's domain from the rest of the bank. Bernard Candler wanted his customers to be able to discuss private financial matters in confidence.

Candler was a man in control of his bank, his town and his life. He didn't like exceptions to that rule. He was facing a big exception now. The two men sitting in front of him had just delivered shocking news.

'Enoch Brighton opposing me for mayor? Why, that's absurd!' Surprise had made the banker's voice even higher-pitched than usual.

'Afraid it's true, Mr Candler,' Rupert Bushrod confirmed. 'There's a big sign in the window of Brighton's Mercantile: ENOCH BRIGHTON FOR MAYOR, IT'S TIME FOR A CHANGE.'

'He even spelled all the words right,' Clarence added. 'I checked 'em with that fancy two-volume dictionary we've never been able to sell.'

'The only people who'll vote against me are the riff-raff.' The banker waved his arms erratically.

'That's absolutely right, Mr Candler.' Rupert's voice was almost a shout.

'Well, of course.' Candler appeared somewhat calmer.

'There's only one problem,' Clarence chimed in.

'Oh?' The banker's calmness began to dissipate.

'The riff-raff make up the majority of the town,' Clarence explained. 'Without their votes, you'll lose the election.'

'That's where we can help you, sir.' Rupert spoke confidently.

'What do you mean?' Suspicion crept into Candler's voice.

'Why, there's no one in this town more trusted by the riff-raff than Clarence and me,' Rupert proudly asserted. 'We play poker with 'em, get drunk with 'em, even let 'em sleep behind our store.'

'Enoch runs 'em off,' Clarence added. 'He won't associate with the town's low lifes. Does Candler want a man like that for mayor?'

'And we can help you with more than just the ne'er-do-wells.'

'I don't follow you, Rupert.' Candler sounded at least a bit interested.

'Well sir, 'bout a year ago we ordered four hundred empty tobacco pouches. We got a great deal on 'em.'

The banker's face crunched up. 'How much demand is there in Candler for tobacco pouches?'

'Good question, sir,' Rupert replied. 'Unfortunately, it's a question we forgot to consider at the time.'

'The experience has been educational, though.' Clarence spoke up cheerfully. 'We've discovered the remarkable number of years one tobacco pouch can last a man. Why, there are men in this town usin' tobacco pouches handed down to them by their granddaddies.'

Bernard rolled his eyes. 'I fail to understand how this—'

'Our mistake will keep you in office, Mr Mayor.' Rupert beamed a confident smile.

'How?'

Rupert's smile grew even wider. 'Clarence and me will place gumdrops and rock candy in those pouches and hand

37

'em out to folks this Saturday. We'll tie a little note to each pouch, "*Candler for Mayor*". All we ask is that you pay for the candy.'

Bernard's face turned red. 'You're suggesting that I stoop to bribing people to vote for me?'

'Absolutely!' Rupert replied. 'My brother and me has studied on it and bribery is a sure thing when it comes to winnin' elections.'

'Well, I suppose it wouldn't hurt.' The banker folded his hands and held them in front of him as if praying.

'That's the spirit, Mr Candler!' Rupert bounded from his chair. 'You jus' concentrate on the bankin' business and let my brother and me do the politikin'. We'll get you the vote of ever' one who likes free candy. You're as good as re-elected.'

Bernard Candler looked more confused than reassured as the two men left his office.

As they walked back to their store the two brothers discussed the meeting.

'We never did ask him direct 'bout what we really want.'

'You gotta understand politiks, Clarence. With us beatin' drums for him and all, Bernard can't very well foreclose on us. It would sure hurt his standin' as a man of the people.'

'But he ain't gonna cancel our debts. . . ?'

' 'Course not, but he'll sorta put 'em on the shelf for a while, give us a chance to reorganize our business.'

'Jus' how we gonna re-or-gan-ize?'

As they arrived at their store both brothers paused and gave it a careful look. After a few moments Rupert replied to his brother's question:

'Well, I thought we might start by sweepin' the floor.'

'Good idea.' Clarence put a hand under his chin and looked thoughtful. 'We can use one of those over-priced brooms we can't sell.'

CHAPTER NINE

Giles Hobart paced about his small office at the church. He eyed the cot standing in one corner. That cot served as his bed but, after returning from the desolation that had been the Scott ranch, he had been unable to sleep.

'Will I ever be able to sleep again?' Giles asked himself out loud.

There was a light tap on the door. A feeling of panic gripped the pastor. Had whoever was outside heard him talking?

He took a few quick steps to his desk and opened the Bible that lay there. He then went to the door and admitted two men.

'Good morning, gentlemen.'

'I'm afraid it ain't been a good morning for Rance and me, Preacher,' Sheriff Clint Mead said. 'We went out to the Scotts' to retrieve Josh's body, like I told ya yesterday we were goin' to.'

Had they found Tillie's hiding place?

'That must have been awful.' Giles spoke as he waved the men into his office.

'Yes, we just left the body with the undertaker.' The lawman pointed to the open Bible. 'Are ya preparin' for the service this afternoon?'

'Ah . . . yes.'

Clint nodded his head. 'Just wanted ya to know that Josh's body is here. Ya can go ahead as planned. Chet will have it ready in a coffin and all in a few hours.'

Chet Wilhelm was the town's barber and undertaker.

The pastor noticed a tin star on Rance's shirt, similar to the one the sheriff was wearing.

'Does Candler have two sheriffs now?'

Both of Hobart's companions gave weak smiles. They weren't sure if the pastor was trying to make a light joke or if the question was genuine.

Mead waved a thumb in Dehner's direction.

'Rance will be in town for a while and has agreed to serve as a volunteer deputy.'

'I plan to help Clint and Boone with making sure nothing happens to Jenny,' Dehner said. 'If you need help with that list of men keeping an eye on the Kaplan residence, feel free to add my name.'

'Thanks, I might do that.'

The sheriff placed a hand on Giles's shoulder. 'We sure appreciate all you're doin' to help us, Preacher.'

Hobart exchanged friendly goodbyes with the two men as they left. He then collapsed into a chair behind his desk. There was a graveside service he had to prepare for. His hands began to shake and for a moment he thought he could hear Tillie's voice.

She was laughing at him.

A circle of people surrounded two large cavities in the grave-yard. A coffin lay beside each empty space. Those coffins would soon be lowered into the ground. But first, the eyes of all those in the circle were on the clergyman who stood by himself, a Bible in hand.

Giles Hobart started to speak but managed only a choking sound. He cleared his throat and tried again.

'I didn't know Josh and Tillie Scott as well as many of you. . . .'

He was lying. Lying as he stood before people who regarded him as a man of God.

'I recall running into the Scotts at Brighton's Mercantile one Saturday. . . .' Hobart continued.

His eyes fell on Sylvia Kaplan who was standing beside Enoch Brighton. *She is such a fine woman. I want to look her in the eye and tell her so many things, but. . . .*

'And, while we were discussing Scripture, Tillie mentioned to me her love for the twenty-third Psalm.'

Another lie. Tillie never mentioned the Bible to me. She knew what kind of man I really am. The pastor began to read:

'The Lord is my shepherd, I shall not want. . . .'

'*So, Giles, you finally got what you really want.*' Those were his exact words. I should have turned away from that twisted, cruel face, the brown, tobacco-stained teeth and whiskey-sodden breath. 'You're a nobody, Giles, no better. . . .'

'Yea, though I walk through the valley of the shadow of death. . . .'

The smile vanished and blood spurted from his lips as I hit him. Suddenly a gun was drawn, there was a scream.

'Surely goodness and mercy shall follow me all the days of my life, and I will dwell in the house of the Lord forever.'

Hobart concluded the reading with a short prayer and the circle of people began to disperse. Giles closed his Bible and began to walk away hurriedly, passing the two gravediggers who were now preparing to go about their day's work.

'Reverend Hobart.'

The pastor stopped and turned as Sylvia Kaplan approached him. The woman's eyes were moist.

'I want to thank you for that beautiful service. You brought all of us a lot of comfort.'

Giles looked around and saw several people standing close by, nodding their heads in agreement with Sylvia's words.

Their appreciation brought him no satisfaction. He wanted to turn and run.

'Thank you,' once again Giles's words came out as a choke and he had to clear this throat, 'but I really don't think I said—'

'Oh, it wasn't what you said,' Sylvia cut in. 'It was how you said it. Grief for the Scotts and concern for Jenny filled your soul. We could see the anguish in your eyes.'

The woman pulled a handkerchief from her pocket and patted the moisture covering her cheeks.

'Thank you, Reverend.' She turned and walked back to Enoch who put his arm around her. Sylvia rested her head against Enoch's shoulder as they walked off together.

Reverend Hobart returned to his church office but the familiar walls brought him no comfort. Could he summon up the courage to return to that horrible place and retrieve the metal case?

The pastor heard a noise coming from outside the door, or thought he did; he couldn't be sure. Cautiously he left his office and entered the sanctuary, as if something there threatened him.

'Get a grip on yourself, man,' he whispered to himself. 'There's nobody here.'

As if to reassure himself of his own words Reverend Hobart began to walk up the middle aisle, carefully looking under the wooden pews. The noise could have been a cat or a critter of some kind that had managed to crawl into the building.

He reached the tenth and final pew, which fronted the small lobby at the entrance to the church. There was nothing there.

The preacher closed his eyes and took a deep breath.

A sensuous feminine voice filled the sanctuary:

'Giles.'

Hobart turned and faced the front of the church. A

ghostly apparition stood in the pulpit.

'Tillie.'

As he spoke the name Hobart took several stumbling steps backward.

The woman's laughter filled the sanctuary, bouncing off the walls in a loud echo as if the building was a stone canyon. Giles pressed his hands against his ears and looked down at the floor.

The laughter morphed into a mocking voice.

'Be sure your sins will find you out.'

'No! Go away.'

Silence followed the clergyman's shouts. Hobart slowly raised his head and looked around. The space behind the pulpit was empty. Except for himself, there was no one present.

Reverend Giles Hobart dropped to his knees and began to cry uncontrollably.

CHAPTER TEN

Boone Logan laughed as he spoke to his companion.

'Buryin's sure do strange things to folks. People came in from the ranches today, acted all sorrowful over Josh and Tillie gettin' planted, now they're drinkin' and carryin' on in the saloons; at least the men are.'

Rance Dehner smiled and nodded. 'I'll let you keep an eye on the mourners. I'm going over to the Kaplan home to check with the man on guard there.'

Logan gave the detective an approving wave and watched him hurry off. Boone liked and respected Dehner but the deputy felt that Clint Mead wasn't giving him a fair try at being a lawman, and having an experienced detective around didn't help matters. From what he had heard, the sheriff had been rough on all of his deputies and had trouble keeping them, but it seemed to Boone that he was being treated worse than most.

'Stop feelin' sorry and do your job,' the deputy whispered to himself. He stopped in front of the Prairie Dog saloon and looked around the town. The place was busier and noisier than usual for a Friday night and the reason wasn't only the funeral that afternoon. His boss had persuaded Bernard Candler and Enoch Brighton to have a political debate in the main street of the town the next morning. That move had inspired every saloon owner in town to start accepting bets on who would win the election.

Boone turned around and looked over the batwings of the Prairie Dog. Two strangers were leaning against the bar. He'd have to do his duty and find out why the strangers were in Candler.

Can't wait till Enoch is mayor, and I won't hafta bother with talkin' to ever' saddle bum that rides through, Logan thought to himself as he stepped into the Prairie Dog.

But as he approached the two strangers, the deputy tensed up. These men were not the usual drifter types. Their guns were tied down low and they both looked like hardcases. One was tall and heavy set while the other, of a wiry build, stood at average height.

Boone smiled as he slipped into the line at the bar. He was now standing beside the wiry newcomer.

'Evenin', gents. The name is Boone Logan.'

The wiry man looked at the badge on Boone's shirt and sneered.

'Now yur expectin' us ta tell ya our names. After that, yur gonna ask us why we're in town and how long we plan to stay.'

Boone was uncertain as to what to do next. His first inclination was to follow the mayor's instructions and tell the men they had one week to find a job but somehow that didn't seem wise.

'Only doin' my job, gents, after all. . . .' The new deputy couldn't quite keep the tension out of his voice.

Wiry picked up on the deputy's nervousness.

'Go do yur job someplace else.'

'Look mister,' this time Logan's voice was firm, 'there's law in this town and—'

'Hey now, men, no sense in getting all riled.' The tall, heavy-set man raised both hands in a calm-down gesture. 'My name is Luke.' He pointed a finger at his companion, 'and this here is Tom. We're jus' passing through, been spending a lot of time in a saddle and that makes Tom a bit ornery. You'll have to forgive him, Deputy.'

'So, ya ain't in town on business.' Boone's voice remained firm.

Luke grinned in an artificial manner.

'The only business we got here is drinking in this saloon and sleeping in the town hotel. We'll be riding out at sunup.'

Tom grumbled something and Luke quickly touched his shoulder. Tom fell silent and Luke continued to prattle on with a lot of friendly assurances.

'Enjoy your time in Candler.' Boone brought the palaver to an end. 'Evenin', gents.' He strolled languidly out of the Prairie Dog.

Once he was on the boardwalk he quickly moved to the alley beside the saloon and positioned himself where he could easily spot anyone who was leaving.

Luke had sure wanted to make peace with him, Logan reckoned. Tom was a hothead and Luke seemed worried his partner might ruin their plans, but what plans?

The deputy thought about fetching Dehner or going back to the sheriff's office and getting Clint Mead. But what would he tell them? Two hardcases were acting strange in a bar?

No. He would handle this himself – if there was anything to handle.

Boone didn't have to wait long to have his suspicions confirmed. Less than ten minutes after the deputy had left the saloon Luke and Tom departed, walking in the opposite direction, away from the hotel.

Logan followed at a reasonable distance behind them. The two hardcases crossed the dirt street and entered the alley between Mason's saddle shop and Brighton's Mercantile.

Both businesses were closed for the day, but Enoch often stayed late in his store, stocking shelves or doing work in the storage room at the back.

Boone ran across the street and into the alley. He was the only person there and he moved quickly to the back corner of Brighton's Mercantile; he could see the back door standing open.

That wasn't unusual, at least not for July. Enoch frequently kept his back door open, hoping for any breeze that might waft through the store. But Boone could hear voices coming through that door: angry voices. That was unusual.

The deputy drew his gun and moved cautiously toward the open doorway. He flattened himself against the back wall of the store and listened to a voice he recognized as belonging to Luke.

'You're gonna do exactly what we tell you, storekeeper.'

Logan peered around the doorframe. Luke was facing Enoch. Both the hardcase and the storekeeper were standing behind a stack of wooden crates that reached to their hips. Tom was leaning against a side wall, away from the crates. His gun was holstered.

'I was never one for takin' orders,' Enoch replied. Logan was sure the storekeeper had spotted him.

'Oh, is that so—'

Enoch's arm moved too fast for both of his tormentors. A hard punch drove Luke backwards, knocking over crates on his fast journey to the floor. Enoch jumped on top of him. Tom froze for a moment before going for his gun.

Boone Logan ran through the doorway but stumbled as he fired his .44. The shot went into the ceiling and Boone had to hit the boards to duck the shot from Tom. The wiry outlaw ran, panicked, from the store.

Boone sprang back onto his feet as he heard Enoch's shout:

'Get that snake, Boone. I'll handle this one.'

Boone Logan ran out the door and around to the main street. To his right he spotted Tom at a hitch rail, mounting a gray, and Rance Dehner running toward him from the direction of the Kaplan house.

Logan fired at the rider who was starting to gallop out of town, then shouted at Dehner.

'Stop him, Rance. That jasper tried to kill Enoch.'

Dehner saw the gun in the escaping outlaw's hand pivot in his direction. The detective pulled his .45 as he dropped to the planks and returned fire as a bullet whistled over him.

Tom screamed in pain and went limp. He struggled to stay atop the gray but quickly folded over and plunged to the ground. After he'd been dragged a few feet Tom's boot came off, leaving him lying in the street as the horse ran off.

The outlaw cried profanities as he reached for the pistol, which now lay only a few feet from him. Dehner had risen onto a knee and kept his weapon pointed at the adversary.

'Don't touch the gun, mister. I won't warn you again.'

More profanities spurted erratically from Tom's mouth as he grabbed the gun. Those were his last words. Dehner's next shot exploded into his head.

The detective approached the fallen outlaw cautiously but the caution was only out of habit. He knew he was walking toward a corpse.

As he went to kneel beside the body Dehner saw Boone Logan hurrying to the back of Brighton's Mercantile and Sheriff Mead running toward the trouble from the direction of his office. The detective quickly joined Mead and the two men took quick steps toward the back of the store.

Reaching the doorway, they saw that Enoch Brighton's face was ashen. He was holding Luke's gun in one hand. Both Clint and Rance looked confused as they entered. Boone Logan seemed to be the only one of the four men who understood what was going on.

'Ya gut-shot him,' the deputy said to Enoch. 'No one could live through a bullet bein' fired that close. Ya musta fired while ya were tryin' to wrestle the gun away from him.'

Enoch nodded his head.

Sheriff Mead spoke in a quiet voice to his deputy:

'Start at the beginnin' and tell us what happened.'

Boone gave a quick summary of events starting with his conversation with the two hardcases in the Prairie Dog. He nodded toward the back door when he came to a certain point in the narrative.

'When Enoch saw me, he took one hell of a gamble. He punched Luke and sent him to knockin' over all the crates before he dropped like a sack of oats. I stumbled over my own big feet when comin' inside to help. . . .'

Dehner was impressed with the deputy's account. Not only did Boone Logan present all the important facts, he didn't try to excuse his own mistakes.

A few moments of silence followed Boone's story. Then Rance broke the quiet.

'Tell me, Enoch, what did Luke order you to do . . . the order you refused?'

The question caused Enoch to look a bit startled, as if he had just been awakened from a nightmare. He looked down at the corpse as if to confirm that what had just happened was real.

'The guy who called hisself Luke, he tol' me to show him where I keep the shotgun.' The storekeeper's voice was little more than a whisper. 'He said there was gonna be an unfortunate accident tonight. The shotgun was gonna go off and kill me.'

Dehner pushed his hat back and grimaced.

'That means those thugs knew you kept a shotgun here as opposed to – let's say – a Winchester or a pistol, and they knew you worked late at the store and kept the back door open.'

'That don't mean much.' Clint Mead shrugged his shoulders. 'Anyone who's been in town a day or two would know those things.'

'But Luke and Tom haven't been in Candler for a day or

two,' Dehner replied. 'They just got in town tonight, unless they were hiding out. The men who just got killed were hired guns. We need to find out who hired them.'

Enoch's voice now took on strength, 'But why kill me?'

'I don't know,' Dehner admitted. 'But it appears that Jenny is not the only one in this town whose life is in danger.'

'Go home and try to get some rest, Enoch.' The deputy nodded toward his companions. 'The sheriff, Rance and me will see to the bodies.'

'That's a good idea.' The sheriff smiled wanly. 'After all, tomorrow is a big day for you, Enoch.'

'Oh, that's right,' Dehner said. 'I remember seeing the signs in the stores.'

'Yep.' The sheriff's voice became buoyant. 'Tomorrow we're havin' a big political debate. I think it's gonna be quite a show.'

CHAPTER ELEVEN

A long buckboard wagon stretched across Candler's main street. Six men were sitting on the wagon in chairs borrowed from the Prairie Dog saloon. On the left side perched Enoch Brighton and beside him was a well-dressed blond-haired man of about thirty. Dehner had never seen him before.

On the right side sat a fidgety Bernard Candler. Sitting beside him were the reasons for his unease: Rupert and Clarence Bushrod.

Sitting between the two camps, his chair a few feet away from both as if to emphasize his neutrality, was Reverend Giles Hobart. The pastor pulled out his timepiece. 'Eleven a.m. sharp. Are you ready, gentlemen?'

After receiving affirmative nods, the clergyman stood up and began to address the large crowd gathered in front of the wagon.

'On behalf of both Enoch Brighton and Bernard Candler I thank you all for coming. One week from today the people of this town will vote for their next mayor. Today, both candidates will stand in front of you and present their cases. Enoch Brighton has won the coin toss and elected to go first and so, Mr Brighton, it is now your turn.'

Loud and enthusiastic applause sounded from the crowd as Enoch Brighton made his way to the center of the wagon and stood in front of Giles Hobart, who had sat back down.

'Ya folks all know me, ya come by the store to buy the things ya need and to jaw. Sometimes, it's just to jaw and ya don't spend no money at all!'

Loud laughter came from the crowd. Enoch laughed along before continuing:

'I know all of ya and I know what you're all goin' through. Now, I'm not much for talkin' in front of a crowd, so I've asked a friend to do my talkin' for me. He just arrived in Candler this mornin' . . . Mr Stephen Montague of the Union West Railroad.'

A scattering of applause accompanied Stephen Montague as he took Enoch's place at the center of the wagon. The railroad rep made an elaborate gesture in Enoch's direction as the storekeeper returned to his chair.

'Ladies and gentlemen, Candler has a very fine citizen in the person of Enoch Brighton.'

That line was intended to draw loud applause and it succeeded. Enoch waved to the crowd as he sat back down. The broad smile on Stephen's face lost some of its gleam as he began his talk.

'As many of you know, the Union West Railroad has a great interest in coming through Candler and building a major depot here. We have tried to talk to your current mayor about our desire but, unlike Enoch, Bernard Candler isn't one for friendly conversation. In fact, the last time some of our people tried to speak with his honour, he told them to go to a place that is even hotter than Candler in the summertime.'

This time people pointed toward Bernard as they indulged in raucous laughter. The banker squirmed. He was obviously not enjoying this demonstration of democracy in action.

'Enoch Brighton is a young man with young ideas for Candler. I strongly recommend you vote for him in next Saturday's election.' Montague waved to the crowd and returned to his chair.

Giles stood up hurriedly.

'Now we will hear from Mayor Candler,' he announced.

Bernard's lips were pressed together as he made his way to the center of the wagon. He gave the crowd a rueful look.

'I've been mayor of this town since it existed. All of you look pretty healthy and prosperous to me and you got that way without a railroad. Mr Montague is a liar, I never told anyone to got to . . . ah . . . I don't talk like that. Ah, now here are two . . . ah . . . gentlemen to speak for me.'

As the mayor returned to his chair, he was almost knocked over by the Bushrod brothers in their haste to reach the center of the wagon.

'I know you folks are all shocked by what ya jus' heard,' Rupert shouted.

'Yep,' Clarence continued, 'ain't no one accused my brother and me of bein' gentlemen before.'

Rupert held up a finger as if he had been struck with an idea.

'I'll bet Mr Candler noticed we both took baths last night and wanted to encourage us to keep actin' civilized.'

Clarence nodded his head. 'Our mayor likes things civilized, that's why he wants to keep out the railroad. A railroad would bring in lots of new riff-raff and make things hard on the riff-raff that's already here. Why, before ya know it, they'd be throwing drunks in jail instead of lettin' 'em sleep it off behind the Bushrod brothers' general store.'

'A great tradition would die.' Rupert shook his head mournfully.

The crowd laughed appreciatively. Rance Dehner chuckled along as he watched from the boardwalk beside the wagon. The detective stood between Clint Mead and Boone Logan. Rance noticed that Boone was enjoying the antics of the Bushrod brothers but Clint looked worried. Dehner reckoned that the sheriff had thought this event would be an absolute triumph for Enoch Brighton. It wasn't quite turning out that way.

'I believe Mr Candler when he says he never told no one to go to the hot place,' Clarence declared pompously.

Rupert picked up the thread.

'He don't hav'ta – why, jus' the way he can glare at ya makes ya wish ya was down below, or any place but standin' where Bernard can see ya. But study on it some and you'll realize Bernard Candler almost never forecloses on no one.'

'That's our mayor,' Clarence agreed. 'He sure knows how ta make a man miserable but he almost never tosses him out in the cold. So, vote for the sourpuss with a heart of gold – or at least silver or maybe copper, but vote for Bernard Candler!'

The crowd responded with both laughter and applause. But were they expressing support for Mayor Candler or gratitude for the antics of the Bushrod brothers? Dehner couldn't tell.

Reverend Hobart once again addressed the throng.

'Both the candidates and their spokesmen will remain in this location to answer any questions you may have. Voting is one of the most vital responsibilities we have as citizens. Please join me in prayer as we ask the Lord for his guidance in the election next week.'

Immediately following Hobart's 'Amen' Enoch Brighton and Stephen Montague hopped off the wagon and began to mix with the crowd, most of whom remained in the street. Smart politics, Dehner thought, chuckling to himself. The action provided a good contrast to the demeanor of Mayor Candler, who had to be helped off the wagon by the Bushrod brothers.

But once Candler was on the ground the crowd seemed to divide their attention evenly between the banker and the storekeeper. Suddenly a boy shouted something Dehner couldn't quite understand and a group of children ran toward the mayor and the Bushrod brothers.

Dehner smiled as he spoke to the deputy standing beside him.

'I'll check in on the situation with his honour; why don't you keep an eye on the crowd around Enoch?'

'Sure thing,' Boone replied.

Rance didn't speak to the sheriff, whose face was red and twisted. But Clint Mead followed behind the detective as he wound his way through the crowd toward Bernard Candler and the Bushrod brothers.

As Dehner drew closer to the action he could hear Clarence speaking loudly while his brother handed out small pouches to the children.

'Yes, folks, here we have absolute proof that Bernard Candler isn't a stingy man. Why, he's givin' free candy to the kids even though not one of them can vote.'

Laughter swelled from the adults as they watched their children snatch up the candy. Clarence's voice became comically pompous.

'But don't you folks worry none, there's no tobacco in them pouches. We don't want our young'uns to get any bad habits and start actin' like their daddies.'

The laughter increased. Bernard, who stood a few feet behind the brothers, even managed a slight grin.

'You Bushrod brothers enjoy makin' a joke out of this election.'

The sheriff's harsh shout silenced the crowd. Both children and adults looked at the lawman with surprise and curiosity, but Clarence maintained his friendly gusto.

'Why, humour has always been a part of American politics, Sheriff. Don't be fooled by those paintin's ya see of George Washington. Why, from what I hear, George was a real cut-up. And once ya got a few drinks into Abe Lincoln, he'd be tellin' stories that had folks laughin' so hard, their sides ached.'

Clarence's reply relaxed the crowd but not for long. Mead pointed an accusing finger at the brothers.

'Last night, two hired guns tried to kill Enoch, one week before the election. You two fellas find that funny?'

Bernard Candler had been more than content to let his spokesmen do the talking, but Mead's interruption caused the banker's body to stiffen as a silent fury came to his face. Candler hastily stepped between the brothers and braked only inches from the lawman.

'Sheriff Mead, I resent your absurd implication. You have demeaned yourself and your office.'

'I didn't imply anything.'

Dehner noted that the glare about which the Bushrod Brothers had been joking was now in Candler's eyes, and Clint Mead appeared intimidated. The sheriff had leaned back a bit as he shouted his response.

Candler's glare intensified.

'You implied that I hired two thugs to murder my opponent in this race. I demand an apology – immediately!'

A large circle had formed around the sheriff and the mayor. Dehner gave the crowd a quick glance and noticed Enoch stretching his neck in order to see the small drama being played out.

Bernard spoke quietly and yet everyone could hear him.

'I am waiting, Sheriff.'

Clint looked at the ground, then stared at his hands for a moment before speaking.

'I mighta' said things in a way that coulda' gave people the wrong notion. I apologize.'

'Apology accepted.' The mayor extended his hand to Clint Mead who nervously accepted it. Rance thought the handshake to be a total victory for Bernard Candler and reckoned the rest of the crowd took it the same way.

'Now that ya both shook hands, I want ya to go to separate corners and when the bell rings come out fightin',' Rupert declared loudly.

'That's boxin',' Clarence said. 'This here is politiks.'

'You mean there's a difference?' Rupert asked.

The crowd laughed and began to move toward Bernard Candler, who seemed to be suddenly enjoying his role as a candidate. Clint walked away with his head down as if looking for a hole to jump into.

Dehner followed behind the lawman and placed a hand on his shoulder.

'You did the right thing by apologizing, Clint.'

Mead stopped and gave a deep sigh. 'I shoulda stayed outta politics. It's jus' that . . . I thought this would be a great day for Enoch and I lost my temper when them Bushrods stole the show. Shouldn't have said what I did; only made things worse for Enoch.'

'Enoch did just fine.' Dehner glanced around him. 'Things look pretty settled here. Can you and Boone do without me?'

'Sure. Whatcha got planned?'

'There's a lot going on in Candler that doesn't quite make sense. I need to ask some questions.'

'Ask all the questions you want.' Mead gave a forced laugh. 'Most of the town is right here.'

'I'm planning on. . . .'

Dehner stopped speaking as he saw Doc Reggie coming toward him. The look on the doctor's face was grim.

Stephen Montague sipped coffee as he stood by a campfire and looked at his horse, which was picketed in a nearby grove of trees. He raised the tin cup in a toast and gave the chestnut a friendly smile.

'Men can gripe about saddle sores all they want. I prefer the sores to having my bones rattled all day while I'm cooped up with strangers on a stagecoach.' He took another drink from the cup. 'Guess the stagecoach will still be around for a

57

while but its days are numbered. Yep, Candler needs the railroad, so do a lot of other towns. Trains are a civilized way to travel.'

Montague wasn't alarmed by the clomping sound which approached the fire. Clouds blocked most of the moonlight but Stephen could make out the familiar figure, which pulled up, dismounted, and placed a few heavy stones on the reins of his horse.

'Right on time, friend; care for some coffee?'

Montague was already pouring java as his question received an affirmative answer. He handed the cup over the camp fire.

'Sorry, but the bottom of that cup leaks just a bit.'

The newcomer laughed and assured him it was no problem.

'Would you like to sit down and relax some?' Montague asked, waving toward the ground.

'No. Can't stay long.'

'I understand,' Stephen replied. 'Say, I hope my joke about Bernard telling the Union West Railroad reps to go to hell didn't foul things up. The joke just came to me while I was speaking. I think most folks understood what I meant, don't you?'

Montague's companion smiled, set his coffee cup on the ground, then drew his gun.

'Why—'

Montague never finished his question. Two bullets in the chest halted his speech and tossed him to the ground, dead.

The killer holstered the gun, then stepped back and placed a hand on his nervous horse to settle him. The steed neighed loudly, as did the chestnut by the grove of trees, but the murderer mused silently to himself that all the noise posed no problem. He had purposely chosen this remote spot for the meeting.

He stooped down and retrieved the tin cup. Montague

made good coffee. He'd like to have a second cup but time didn't allow. He needed to plant Stephen Montague in an unmarked grave, destroy the campfire, turn the chestnut loose, and get back to town before anyone missed him.

CHAPTER TWELVE

The Sunday evening service at the First Church of Candler was followed by groups of people forming circles in front of the church and engaging in lively discussions concerning the political event of the day before. Both candidates drifted from one circle to the next, as did the Bushrod brothers.

Dehner could hear Rupert's voice.

'Me and my brother will probably be runnin' ourselves, someday,' he was declaring loudly,

'You two are going to run for office?' a shocked female voice exclaimed.

'No ma'am, we'll be runnin' out of town when somebody finally buys that jerky we've had layin' around for a hundred years and tries to eat it.'

Dehner heard this exchange from a distance. He was in a small group of people who were walking with Doc Reggie toward his home. Reginald Dalrymple's face appeared grim, as it had the day before.

'I want to keep this . . . attempt to help Jenny . . . a secret if possible,' the doctor said. 'I've asked Sylvia to be present because she has accepted the responsibility of raising the child. Enoch could have come because . . . never mind . . . he's busy with his political duties.'

An awkward pause followed. Dalrymple had almost said that Enoch would probably marry Sylvia and thus become

Jenny's father but stopped himself when he realized there had been no official announcements in that regard.

Doc Reggie quickly ended the pause.

'I've asked Mr Dehner along because he was the first person we know of to find Jenny after she retreated into silence. Sheriff Mead, I think you should witness these events as the upholder of our town's law. And Reverend Hobart, you are needed for your spiritual insights.'

Sylvia Kaplan tightened her hold on Jenny's hand as the group continued its journey to Doc Reggie's house.

'I'm still worried that we are doing something very wrong. Hypnosis belongs in a medicine show, if it belongs anywhere. There's something evil about it.'

'I understand your anxiety, Miss Kaplan,' Giles said. 'Hypnosis has been exploited by many scoundrels interested only in a fast dollar. But, from my years at college in the East, I can assure you that hypnosis can be a legitimate medical tool.'

Sylvia appeared calmed by the pastor's words and Rance wondered if Hobart's reference to the East was the reason. Sylvia Kaplan spent six days a week in Brighton's Mercantile. As yet, Candler did not have a ladies' shop but Brighton's had a selection of women's hats, bonnets and even a few dresses. All of these items came with the assurance of representing the latest fashion from the East.

The West was a vital, robust land of curious contradictions, the detective silently mused. Westerners prided themselves on their fierce independence and freedom from traditions, yet they cast an occasional eye eastward, seeking assurance that they were behaving themselves correctly.

'Giles is right.' Doc Reggie kicked a stone as he spoke. 'And we desperately need the tool of hypnosis. So far, Jenny hasn't responded to a thing any of us has done to make her speak. She eats a little bit and sleeps. Toys don't interest her. She won't talk or even make meaningful gestures. If we let this situation go on much longer I'm afraid Jenny will never come back to us.'

'But why do this at your house, Doc?' Clint sounded irritated. He had expressed strong doubts about hypnotism when the doctor first mentioned the subject the day before. 'Wouldn't it be better to do it in the Kaplan home where the girl might feel more comfortable?'

Sylvia gave the lawman a chagrined look.

'Hypnosis makes my mother even more jumpy than it makes me. I don't like going behind my mother's back, but. . . .'

As they ascended the steps that fronted the doctor's house a huge creature began to raise itself up on the porch to greet them.

'Goliath, sit!' Doc Reggie snapped his command, afraid that the dog would jump on the child and scare her. The animal obeyed his owner.

But Goliath did not frighten Jenny. The girl ran up the stairs and embraced the dog around his neck.

The adults walked cautiously toward Jenny and Goliath, as if observing some sacred ritual they couldn't quite understand. Sylvia spoke in a stage whisper:

'This is the first time Jenny has responded so strongly to anything since that day Mr Dehner brought her to the store.'

'I should have remembered,' Doc Reggie replied in a slightly louder voice, 'every time I saw the Scotts in town Jenny would always make a fuss over Goliath and ask to play with him.'

Goliath licked the little girl's face. Jenny's face remained empty of emotion but she petted her friend. Doc Reggie crouched beside his patient.

'We're going inside my house now, Jenny. Would you like for Goliath to come with you?'

Jenny nodded her head.

The doctor took the girl's hand and led her into the

house. The rest of the group stepped quietly behind them as if afraid that by making too much noise they would break a spell. Inside, it became obvious Doc Reggie had prepared his living room for the strange procedure that was about to occur. A large comfortable armchair stood in the middle of the room with a lamp perched on a table beside it. A pale gleam of moonlight came through the room's large front window.

Doc Reggie led the little girl to the chair.

'Make yourself comfortable, Jenny.' He motioned for the dog to sit beside the chair. 'You can keep one hand on Goliath, if you'd like.'

The moment Jenny had settled into the armchair she placed a hand on Goliath's head. Doc Reggie lifted the chimney from the lamp, lighted the wick, and set the chimney back in place.

'Goliath adds a new wrinkle to our situation,' he said. 'A subject for hypnosis is not supposed to be distracted. My dog is a bit of a distraction but he relaxes the child, which is also important.'

The doctor looked at the half-circle of people surrounding him. 'This may take a while; all of you need to remain quiet. Ah, Sheriff, could you close those front curtains please?'

The room was now entirely dark except for a patch of light from the lamp, which covered Jenny, Goliath and the doctor. Reggie went down on his knees. His eyes were directly in line with Jenny's.

The doctor spoke in a calm monotone.

'Jenny, I want you to look directly at my forehead. Keep your eyes on my forehead.'

Rance couldn't tell if Jenny was obeying the command or not. Since he had met her the child had always appeared to be in a trance of some kind. Dehner's eyes scanned the rest of the audience to this bizarre procedure. From what he could tell in the dark, everyone else's eyes were locked on Jenny.

'Jenny, your toes are feeling very heavy,' Doc Reggie continued. 'It's almost like your toes are dropping into the ground. . . .'

Reggie spoke similar words to the child about her ankles, legs and arms. At one point, Jenny's arm dropped away from Goliath, her eyes closed and her body went limp.

Dehner noted a tension in Dalrymple's voice as the doctor moved to the purpose of the hypnotism.

'Jenny, you are now thinking back to last Thursday. You are having breakfast. What did you eat for breakfast?'

'Eggs.'

'What else?'

'Biscuits.'

'What else?'

'Gravy and ham.'

'Who is sitting at the table with you, eating breakfast?'

'Mommie and Daddy.'

'Jenny, that morning some visitors came to your house—'

A loud, piercing scream came from the child. Her eyes opened and flamed with terror.

'Starz falling! Starz falling!'

Doc Reggie was shocked and confused. 'Jenny, think back to—'

The little girl screamed again as she looked down at the floor. Sylvia began to approach Jenny.

'Doctor, you must end this,' she protested. Doc Reggie blocked her path with his arm.

'I hope to. . . .'

Jenny had closed her eyes and was now lying back, limp in the chair. Her breathing was heavy.

Sylvia looked directly at the doctor, her voice was firm.

'End it!'

The doctor nodded his head.

'Jenny, it is now Sunday night. You are in my house with your friends – including Goliath. Goliath wants you to pet him. When I snap my fingers you will remember nothing about what just happened. You will want to pet Goliath.'

Dalrymple snapped his fingers. Jenny's eyes opened and she immediately began to pet the dog. Her face was once again expressionless.

'That was awful.' Sylvia's hand shook as she accepted a handkerchief from Giles Hobart and began to dab at her eyes. 'I will not allow you to hypnotize Jenny again, Doctor. Never!'

'Yes, of course, Sylvia, I understand.' A stoic expression of gray disappointment filled Doc Reggie's face as he sprang up from his crouch.

Dehner tried to lighten the somber mood.

'We have made some important progress in helping Jenny tonight,' he suggested.

Sylvia gave him a hard, questioning glare.

Rance pointed at the dog.

'Goliath. Jenny responded to Goliath, she even shook her head for yes when Doc Reggie asked her if she wanted the dog to come into the house with her.'

'Rance has got a point; Goliath may do a lot more to help Jenny than I ever will.' The doctor looked at Sylvia with a pleading expression. 'Please allow me to walk you and Jenny home tonight. I want you to keep Goliath. We need to discuss ways you can use the dog to help Jenny out of this terrible trap she's in.'

The young woman smiled sweetly. 'Yes, Doc Reggie, I'm grateful for all the help you can give. I am sorry for the way I spoke to you tonight, it's just. . . .'

'I understand.'

The group paraded out of the doctor's house. While they were on the porch Sylvia handed Hobart's handkerchief back to him and mouthed a thank you. She then walked off, with

Jenny on one side of her and Doc Reggie on the other. Goliath walked directly beside the child, his tail wagging in apparent optimism.

The other three men remained standing on the porch. Giles Hobart expressed what was in all of their minds.

'When Jenny shouted about stars falling I think that meant something. It related to what happened on that terrible day. But we're certain the Scotts were attacked after sunup; there wouldn't have been any stars in the sky.'

Sheriff Mead pulled out a tobacco pouch from his shirt pocket and a pipe from the pocket in his pants.

'Way I see it, this hypnosis stuff is a lotta' bull.' He returned the tobacco to his shirt pocket. Dehner observed that the lawman was wearing the same shirt he'd had on on the day Dehner first arrived in town with Jenny.

'The hypnosis seems to have left us with more questions than answers.' Dehner tugged at his earlobe. 'I need to go back to the Scott ranch tomorrow morning and do some looking around. Tell me, Sheriff, do you know of any people who've bought horses from the Scotts?'

The lawman ran a match against the porch's railing and sucked the flame into his pipe.

'You're lookin' at one of them. Though I sure didn't keep Josh and Tillie in riches they gave me a discount; said it was 'cause they appreciated the work I do. I know for a fact they gave horses free to some folks who didn't have two coins to rub together. That was the kind of folks the Scotts were.'

Rance turned to the pastor. 'Did you buy a horse from the Scotts or know of anyone who did?'

'Ah, no . . . no to both questions,' Giles seemed shocked by Rance's words, 'but I've never even thought of asking anyone about where they bought their horse.'

'Need to get back to the office.' Mead waved his pipe in a goodbye gesture. 'Poor Boone, he knows nothin' about this hypnotism stuff but he can tell somethin's goin' on tonight and is feelin' ornery because he got left out.'

'I'd tell him everything about tonight,' Dehner advised. 'But tell him to keep it all a secret. No sense in upsetting Sylvia's mom and a lot of other people.'

'You're right,' the sheriff replied as he walked down the porch steps. 'Boone can keep a secret – and folks have enough to worry about. Goodnight.'

As the three men left the doctor's house Dehner watched Giles Hobart carefully. The pastor's steps meandered as he walked back to the church. On a few occasions he stumbled over his own feet.

Giles Hobart entered the church and noticed his hands shaking as he closed the doors.

'Why is Dehner going back to the Scott ranch tomorrow?' he asked the empty pews. 'He said he needed to do some "looking around". That could mean anything.'

Be sure your sins will find you out. . . .

He had thought a return trip to the ranch might not be needed. After all, what were the chances people would find the trapdoor? That metal box would stay buried—

'No!' This time his voice was a shout. 'I haven't gone back because I'm afraid, afraid of ghosts, afraid. . . .'

Hobart fell silent as he inhaled deeply and tried to calm himself. There was only one answer to his dilemma. He had to return to the Scott ranch tonight and face whatever ghosts might be waiting for him: ghosts that were a product of his own delusions.

Yes, tonight he would retrieve the metal case and then everything would be fine.

CHAPTER THIRTEEN

Giles Hobart tethered his horse to the ground beside the Scott ranch, as close to the trapdoor as possible. He had to keep his buckskin nearby. The metal case was heavy. He'd pull it up from where Tillie had hidden it underground and drag it to the horse. He'd then have to lift the case and tie it onto his saddle. With most of the town asleep, he'd be able to ride into Candler without anyone noticing the case.

Or so he hoped. . . .

Hobart looked around as he put a match to his lantern. The coyotes were gone. They had found what they wanted in the ruins and moved on. The pastor trembled as his thoughts wandered to what Josh Scott's body must have looked like after the wild creatures had feasted on it.

He shook his head and inhaled deeply. If he lost control now he would run and never come back.

Giles removed a coiled rope from his saddle and placed it like a necklace around his neck. He then carried the lantern to the trapdoor. He placed the light onto the ash-covered floor, once again pried out the nails that held down the rag rug, and pulled open the door. A wolf howled in the distance as Giles, lantern in one hand, made his way down the ladder to the underground hideout.

He purposely left the trapdoor open. An eerie splatter of

white descended to the ground below. Reaching the final rung, Hobart cautiously stepped off the ladder and watched the whiteness waver as clouds passed over the moon.

'It looks like a ghost,' he whispered.

The pastor then chastised himself. 'Stop the superstitious nonsense!'

Giles knew he had to work fast. He didn't want to take a chance of someone coming along and seeing him at the Scott ranch. And the sun came up early in summer. He needed to get back to town while he still had the cover of night.

Giles took two steps away from the ladder and dropped to his knees. With the moonlight coming down from above and resting on him, the pastor suddenly thought about the Christian martyrs who, throughout the centuries, had prayed while languishing in underground dungeons. Now he was in a pit, digging up evidence that could humiliate him with the goal of destroying it and living a lie.

What will you say, Hobart, when you encounter those martyrs in the afterlife?

Reverend Hobart cried as he dug with his hands. The tears stopped when he came to the metal case he had buried three days before. He removed the rope from around his neck and tied one end to the handle of the case. With the other end of the rope and the lantern in one hand he made his way up the ladder.

The pastor hurried to his buckskin, where he tied the rope around the horn of the horse's saddle. He grabbed the animal's reins.

'Easy boy, just a few steps should do it.'

He backed the horse away from the house, hoping the rope could hold. He had only the word of Clarence Bushrod that the rope was unusually strong. *Yes sir, Preacher, this here is the strongest rope made. And all that dust it's been collectin' on the shelf makes it stronger still.*

Giles had paid two pennies more for the rope at the Bushrod brothers' general store than he would have at Brighton's Mercantile. But at Brighton's Sylvia might have asked him why he needed the rope and he hadn't wanted to lie to her. Not that Sylvia really cared. . . .

A loud thump caused a surge of joy in the pastor. His plan had worked! The case was above ground.

Giles Hobart was a bookish man with no skills when it came to any task except writing and oratory. He often felt humiliated when around a craftsman or, for that matter, any man who could use a hammer and saw or even a plow.

Giddy laughter emanated from the pastor as he ran to the evidence of his triumph. Yes, the case was right there: proof that he could do something else besides preach. Hobart closed the trapdoor and didn't bother to return the nail to where it had helped hold down the rag rug that covered the door. Let Rance Dehner or anyone else discover the secret hideaway. There would be nothing there to incriminate Giles Hobart. He began to pull on the rope, moving the heavy case toward his horse. Not easy work but he could do it.

Hobart paused and gave the lock on the case a careful look. He had to know what Tillie had hidden inside that case. Most of it probably had nothing to do with him. It would be stuff he could dump into the ashes; he need only take away the material that condemned him.

Hobart didn't usually carry a gun, but then he didn't usually creep through a burnt house in night's darkest hours. He pulled a small pistol from a shoulder holster and fired at the lock. The pastor's joy and confidence began to ebb. He had not only missed the lock, he had missed the entire case.

For his second attempt he took a few steps closer to the target. He used his left arm to steady the right as he took careful aim.

'Good evening, Reverend Hobart, or should I say good

morning? Maybe I can help you with that lock.'

Giles turned toward the figure that approached him from out of the darkness.

CHAPTER FOURTEEN

'Mr Dehner, I'm surprised to see you.'

'Obviously.'

Giles Hobart's joy and confidence vanished. He felt small and tawdry.

'I know this looks a bit strange but, you see, I couldn't get to sleep and started thinking . . . ah. . . .'

'What did you start thinking?'

'You yourself said there was a need to come out and take another look at the ranch.'

'And so you came out in the dead of night. What did you expect to find?'

'Well. . . .'

'Reverend Hobart, be an honest man; you're no good at deception. At Doc Reggie's house tonight, I said I was coming out here to have a look around. Your face went ashen. I followed you and could hear you talking to yourself in the church. The conversation sounded tortured. You preach about truth, Pastor, now it's time to own up to it.'

Hobart stared down at his gloved hands. They were covered with dirt. He inhaled slowly before speaking.

'I used to be an associate pastor at a large church in Denver.'

'Yes.'

'An old friend – well, someone I knew while going to

school in the East, looked me up.'

'Was he a pastor too?'

'No, he had studied law and was opening up a law office in Denver. His first name was Raymond and he was an atheist, the kind of non-believer who enjoys mocking the faith. I was trying to convert him but I'm afraid it sort of worked the other way around.'

'What do you mean?'

'Raymond suggested we have dinner at the King's Palace. It was a large establishment in Denver with a dubious reputation. There was gambling and, well. . . .'

'Prostitution.'

'Yes.' Giles again looked down at his hands. 'I shouldn't have gone – but, well – I did. While we were there I spotted Tillie. She was the most beautiful woman I had ever seen. I couldn't take my eyes off her.'

'Did Raymond notice your interest in Tillie?'

'I didn't think so at first. After dinner I ordered dessert while Ray decided to try his luck – or at least that's what he said. He headed in the direction of the roulette wheel, promised he wouldn't be gone long.'

'Go on.'

'While I was by myself, eating a slice of pie, Tillie came and sat down beside me.'

Giles's face contorted and he mumbled a few incoherent words followed by: 'I can't believe I was so stupid.'

'Most men have been stupid at one time or the other over a beautiful woman.' Dehner spoke softly. 'What happened next?'

'Tillie claimed she could tell I was different from most of the men that came to the King's Palace. I told her I was a pastor and I was there to reach out to sinners.'

Giles Hobart began to cry. Dehner said nothing. Hobart's soul was tormented and nothing the detective could say would change that.

The tears stopped. The pastor pressed his lips together, and then continued:

'Tillie said she needed to have a serious discussion with a man of God. She asked me to come up the stairs with her to her room.'

'But when you got to the room, you and Tillie did a lot more than have a discussion.'

'Yes. Afterwards I was confused . . . I stumbled down the stairs and out of the King's Palace. Outside, Raymond was waiting. Of course, he had paid Tillie to . . . he began to mock me in the most vile language imaginable.

'I hit him. He stumbled backwards and pulled a gun. I couldn't believe it. I didn't know he had a gun. I ran at him and grabbed the pistol – or tried to. . . . It fired and Raymond went down.'

'Was he seriously hurt?'

'No, thank God, the bullet just grazed his leg. But the police were called and several newspaper reporters showed up.'

'You found yourself involved in a scandal?'

'Some scandal! The newspapers turned it all into a big joke. You should have seen the headlines.' Hobart lifted his arms upward and seemed to wave them across the sky. ' "Pistol Packin' Preacher Shoots Rival For Soiled Dove".'

'But that's not what happened.'

'I know.' Giles dropped his arms. 'I think the reporters knew too, but they had a funny story that sold newspapers.'

'Did you lose your job at the church?'

'No. The senior pastor thought booting me would make the church look stern and unforgiving. Besides, people wanted to see the man they were reading so much about. My boss did recommend I look for a position elsewhere. But I stayed long enough to have one more meeting with Tillie.'

Rance's eyebrows lifted. 'You didn't go back to the King's Palace?'

'No. Tillie came to me. There was such elegance to that woman's beauty, such graciousness to her manners that no one at the church had any idea who she was when she arrived one day and asked to see me.'

'I suspect she didn't remain gracious when the two of you were alone in your office.'

Giles cringed before continuing: 'Tillie threatened that if I ever revealed she was the soiled dove in the newspaper stories she'd destroy me.'

'How?'

'Tillie claimed she kept a journal, a very extensive journal. She had the names of prominent politicians and business-men who had used her services. If I caused her any trouble she would blackmail those men to see I got run out of the country. This journal was kept under a trapdoor next to her bed.'

'Did she also threaten Raymond?'

'Probably.' Giles shrugged his shoulders. 'I really don't know. I never saw Ray again. According to the papers, he left town shortly after the . . . incident. Of course, I promised Tillie I'd never mention her name to anyone. When she left the office that day I thought I had seen the last of her. If only. . . .'

Hobart told Rance the story of how he had spotted Tillie in the congregation during his first Sunday at the First Church of Candler and how she had threatened him if he revealed her background.

'She told me about still practicing her old habits. That's why I looked for a trapdoor beside the place where her bed had been.'

Coyotes indulged themselves in a string of howls as the detective took in everything he had just been told, but the animals had ceased their noise when Dehner spoke again.

'Did you recognize Tillie's husband, Josh?'

'At first I wasn't positive, but yes, I'm pretty sure I saw him at the King's Palace that terrible night. He appeared to be a professional gambler but I think he was more than that. I think he owned the place.'

'Does anyone else in Candler know about what happened to you at the King's Palace?'

'One,' Giles answered. 'Bernard Candler: he's the main deacon at the church and the man who interviewed me for the job. I felt I had to tell him. He thanked me for my honesty and said that every man deserves a second chance. He has never told anyone else and advised me never to do so either.'

'Does Bernard know Tillie was the woman you were involved with at the King's Palace?'

'Ah, come to think of it, no he doesn't.' The question seemed to surprise Hobart. 'He came to Denver to interview me. Of course, I didn't know Tillie lived in Candler.'

Rance once again went silent, this time without an accompanying chorus of coyotes.

'What are you thinking, Mr Dehner?'

'A lot of random thoughts I need to bring together somehow.' The detective drew his gun and aimed at the lock on the metal case.

'Let's have a look at exactly what Tillie has been hiding.'

CHAPTER FIFTEEN

Dehner holstered his smoking gun and crouched over the case. He removed what was left of the lock and tossed it aside before opening the metal lid.

'Stones!' Giles shouted.

'Yes,' Dehner agreed. 'The case is full of them. Tillie didn't want anyone to run off with her treasure.'

The detective carefully lifted the treasure from where it rested on a bed of rocks. 'Tillie not only maintained a journal, she kept a lot of items stuffed inside it.'

Looking over Dehner's shoulder, Hobart had not, at first, spotted the journal.

'Tillie wasn't lying!' His voice almost rang with relief.

The pastor picked up the lantern and held it near Dehner as the detective lifted himself back up and began to pull some newspaper clippings from the journal. He looked at the stories cut out from the *Rocky Mountain News*. All of them were lurid accounts of the Pistol-Packin' Preacher.

Rance handed the clippings to Giles Hobart.

'I'll let you decide what to do with these.'

Dehner had expected Hobart to rip up the newspaper stories and toss them into the surrounding ashes. That didn't happen. As the pastor carefully looked over the newspaper accounts his face turned solemn. The stories were false, and yet he seemed to feel they contained something important that he could glean from them. Hobart gently folded the clippings and placed them in the pocket of his coat.

Dehner took a large brown envelope from the journal and carefully pulled out the contents. His voice and face both indicated shock.

'Six pictures! Every one of them shows Tillie smiling as a man leers at her while he has one arm around her waist or shoulder.'

'And all of the men look drunk.' Hobart pointed at one of the photos. 'Isn't that Senator. . . ?'

'Yes it is, and he may be running for president in the next election.' Dehner pointed at another picture. 'That's a prominent businessman who lives in Chicago. If this picture were made public it would—'

'He'd become a laughing stock across the country.'

'You were right, Reverend,' Dehner said. 'Josh must have owned the King's Palace. He and Tillie had a very sophisticated operation going. There must have been a room set up for taking a picture at any time. Tillie would lure prominent gents into that room and have a picture taken, which could then be used to bring on some very influential help whenever it was needed.'

'I guess I was a very small fish to them. They didn't take a picture of me.'

'But I'm sure you're in the journal, just in case you became a prominent churchman someday.' Dehner nodded his head at the journal. 'I suspect these pages contain some familiar names and some not so familiar. All of the entries are carefully dated.'

'Tillie changed over time, I know she did.' Hobart shook his head as if trying to shoo away everything in the journal. 'That woman genuinely loved Jenny. She wanted to be a good mother to the child.'

Dehner reflected briefly on the power that Tillie Scott had over men. She had humiliated Giles Hobart and later had threatened him, and yet he defended her character. The woman had obviously made a similar impact on many other men. Rance briefly wished he had met Tillie, then reckoned perhaps it was just as well he had only known her in death.

'I'm sure Tillie did love her little girl, Reverend Hobart. She and Josh were trying to provide a normal life for her . . . in a way. . . .'

'I don't follow you.'

'Josh and Tillie were involved in gambling and prostitution. In most places both practices are illegal but still allowed. The law looks the other way. As a result, folks who come out of gambling and prostitution often have some strange notions about what is normal. They tend to be cynical people who see the law as something to be manipulated.'

'But Josh and Tillie were running a successful horse ranch.'

Dehner gave the pastor a quizzical look. 'How do you know it was successful?'

'Well, Sheriff Mead got his horse from them.'

'Yes, and they gave the sheriff a discount. They also gave away some horses to people who were down on their luck.'

'So, all that is to the good.'

'Maybe not,' the detective said. 'I think the Scotts were making a few public showings about running a horse ranch. It was all a cover.'

'But. . . ?'

'This evening I turned your face the color of snow when I said I was coming out here to look around. And I will come back after the sun is up. But I'm sure I'll find what I saw the first time around – or, to be more accurate, what I didn't find. There weren't any signs that this place was a horse ranch. I couldn't even spot much in the way of dried-up droppings.'

Giles Hobart sighed and looked at the ashes surrounding him.

'What do you think they were doing?'

'I don't know but we need to find out. There are some very bad things happening in Candler, Reverend, and they are all connected somehow.'

'Please call me Giles, and I'll call you Rance.' Hobart smiled at the detective. 'I'd like to be on a first-name basis with the man who has done so much for me.'

'Sure, but I haven't done anything for you.'

'Telling you about my past has vanquished some ghosts. And I am speaking literally. My mind was so plagued by guilt that I actually thought the ghost of Tillie was haunting me. But. . . .'

'What is it, Giles?'

'Until we find out what Tillie and Josh were really up to I guess her ghost will continue to haunt me in a way.'

Dehner nodded in agreement.

'Right now, she's haunting the entire town,' he said.

CHAPTER SIXTEEN

After leaving Giles Hobart at the church Rance grabbed a few hours of sleep in his hotel room, then had a quick breakfast at the hotel's restaurant. After eating he returned to the Scott ranch but his earlier words proved vindicated. He could find nothing to suggest that the Scotts had used their ranch to raise horses.

On his way back into town Rance chatted with his own horse, a habit he had long ceased trying to break.

'The Scotts probably didn't entertain many guests. They did their socializing in town. I'll bet they had several reasons they could give to unexpected visitors for there not being many horses around.'

That afternoon Rance received some good news while doing a round as a volunteer deputy. Sylvia's face was beaming as Dehner stepped into Brighton's Mercantile.

'Doc Reggie's advice has worked.'

'What advice was that?' Dehner looked confused.

The young woman placed a small stack of newspapers in a rack standing a few feet to the side of the counter.

'He told me to have Jenny take over the responsibilities for caring for Goliath, have her feed him, make a bed for him at night, that sort of thing.'

'How's it working out?'

'Wonderful! This morning Jenny spoke her very first

words since losing her parents: "Time to feed Goliath break-fast." I was so excited.'

'Has she said anything since?'

'No. But I can't wait for Goliath's supper time.'

They were both chuckling at Sylvia's last remark when Enoch, Jenny and Goliath stepped through a door at the back of Brighton's Mercantile. With one hand resting on Goliath, Jenny followed Sylvia as she stepped behind the counter.

Dehner smiled broadly at the child.

'I hear you're taking good care of your friend.'

Keeping her hand on the dog, Jenny remained silent.

'She's still very shy.' Sylvia gave Rance an apologetic smile before turning to her boss. 'Has that backroom been cleared out yet?'

'Gettin' there.' Enoch slapped Dehner on the back and spoke in a mock whisper. 'I jus' sleep back there and let the kid do all the work.'

That led to more chuckles but the detective noted that Jenny was not taking part in the fun. As his gaze met that of the little girl, her face went pale and she began to hug Goliath.

Rance wondered whether he evoked bad memories in the child. After all, they had first encountered each other on the day Jenny's parents were murdered.

Enoch motioned for the detective to join him on the boardwalk outside the store. Once they were away from Sylvia and Jenny Enoch's smile vanished and he lowered his voice.

'I know ya'd like for us to keep it secret-like that the girl is gettin' better.'

'That's impossible in a town this small.' Dehner waved the notion off with his hand.

' 'Fraid so,' Enoch agreed. 'But don'tcha worry, I'm keepin' a close eye on the kid.'

Enoch was smiling again when he re-entered the store, but he had to work at it.

*

Rance's mind ran over everything he had learned since arriving in Candler as he made languid steps toward the telegraph office. While he was still a fair distance from his destination he spotted Clint Mead coming out of the office with a piece of paper in his hand and a grim look on his face. Dehner didn't approach the lawman, who hadn't noticed him and had obviously just received some serious if not bad news. The detective figured he would hear about it soon enough.

As Dehner entered the telegraph office the operator, a tall, thin, middle-aged man gave him an anxious smile.

'You received a reply to your telegram to the Lowrie Detective Agency in Dallas.'

The operator had obviously not dispatched many messages to a detective agency and was enjoying the excitement. Rance thanked him as he took the reply, which had been sent by his boss, the owner of the agency, Bertram Lowrie. As usual Lowrie had been thorough in his response.

Dehner gave the operator a humorless smile.

'I suppose a man in your line of work understands the importance of discretion.'

'Dis – what?'

'You know how to keep your mouth shut.'

'Oh . . . ah . . . yep . . . you've got nothing to worry about there.'

Dehner didn't believe him. He was worried. The detective pulled a greenback from his pocket and handed it to the operator.

'This is in appreciation for your silence.' Rance held up the telegram. 'If anyone else in town finds out about this, I'll be paying you a visit and it won't be social.'

The operator's entire body did a nervous twitch. 'You can count on me to be dis . . . I'll keep my mouth shut.'

The detective felt low and ashamed as he left the operator and headed for the sheriff's office. Threatening normally harmless people was an occasional demand of his calling but he didn't like it. Schoolyard bullies were bad enough in school.

Dehner stopped in the middle of the street and jumped back as a horse galloped by him. The rider pulled up in front of the sheriff's office, twirled the black's reins around the hitch rail and ran inside.

The detective also ran. Whatever was going on couldn't wait.

As he stepped quickly into the office Clint Mead and his deputy were trying to calm a young cowboy with reddish-brown hair and matching freckles. They weren't succeeding.

'I don't want no coffee,' the newcomer shouted at Boone Logan. 'Ain't got time for it.'

Sheriff Mead held up both palms as he stood behind his desk.

'Woody, I want ya to take a deep breath, then start from the beginnin' and tell us what happened.'

Woody followed the lawman's instructions but when he spoke his words collided together.

'You know my brother, Jake?'

Mead nodded his head as Boone set the coffee pot back on the stove.

'He's always been crazy but he ain't bad, not really.'

'Has Jake done somethin' to make Herb Brawley mad?'

Boone Logan took a few steps toward Dehner and whispered: 'Herb Brawley owns a ranch a few miles from here. Woody and Jake work for him.'

'He done something to make Brawley mad all right.' Woody answered Mead's question in a shout. 'Before sunup he stole Brawley's Morgan.'

Clint Mead lifted both of his arms to heaven.

'That's the finest horse in this area, it's Herb's pride and joy.'

'Not anymore it ain't,' Woody said. 'The cook saw Jake riding off and woke ever' one up. Brawley led a – a posse, I guess you'd call it, and they caught up with my brother. He didn't get far. The Morgan fell and broke its leg.'

'Oh no.' Mead closed his eyes.

'Yep,' Woody said. 'Brawley had to shoot the horse right there. He brought Jake back to the ranch and plans to hang him. He's letting the men eat breakfast first. They didn't have a chance to eat before – they had to jump outta their bunks and ride out after my fool brother.'

'Let's hope they're slow eaters.' Clint turned to his deputy. 'You keep an eye on the town. Rance; we need to ride fast.'

CHAPTER SEVENTEEN

While riding toward Herb Brawley's Circle B ranch, Dehner noticed the difference between his two companions. Woody's face reflected panic. Sheriff Clint Mead appeared angry. Dehner figured that the sheriff had a tough enough job keeping a town safe and trying to solve the murder of the Scotts. Now, a band of fools were making his job even tougher.

'We might be too late.' Woody pulled up his horse as they approached the ranch. 'I don't see nobody around . . . I know where they've gone.'

'Where?' Mead demanded.

'A cottonwood jus' east of here; that's where the boss man does all the hangin's.'

'You mean Brawley hangs men whenever he gets the notion?' Dehner asked.

'He don't do it regular like, jus' now and agin.'

'Take us to the cottonwood,' Clint ordered.

Their horses were tired but still managed a fast gallop. They didn't have much further to go. Within a few minutes they could hear a man's frantic screams.

'I brung the law,' Woody shouted as they rode up to a clearing where ten men were moving about in an artificially

86

calm manner around a large tree. Most of them turned and seemed to take an interest in the newcomers while expressing no emotion. A small bantam rooster of a man was giving orders as a rope was tossed over a heavy tree branch and a prisoner with his hands tied was being lifted onto a horse. A large overweight gent watched the proceedings with a Sharps-Borchardt .45 rifle in his hands.

As the three newcomers pulled up Sheriff Mead shouted at the bantam rooster.

'What's goin' on here, Herb?'

'Nothin' that concerns you.'

'I think maybe it does.' The sheriff's horse began to blow and the lawman used it as an opportunity to change his approach. 'Sorry about your Morgan, Herb . . . a mighty fine animal.'

'Thanks, Clint, that's good of you.'

The mood seemed to soften. Dehner reckoned that Herb and Clint, while not close friends, had known each other for years and shared the comradeship of men who had lived hard lives in a hard land.

Mead pointed at the man on horseback with his hands tied in front of him.

'I unnerstand this fool ain't the first jasper whose neck you stretched.'

Brawley shrugged his shoulders. 'Only two others; one I caught trying to break into my safe, the other shot another one of my hands in the back 'cause of an argument over a female. You were outta town both times and you always order your deputy not to leave Candler when you're gone, so I handled it myself.'

'I appreciate it, Herb, but times are changin'.' The sheriff patted his horse's neck, then he continued: 'We gotta do stuff closer to the letter of the law.'

Brawley's voice took on an edge.

'One more fool kickin' his feet in the air ain't gonna hurt

that law of yours none.'

The man holding the Sharps-Borchardt grabbed at the chance to shatter the good will between his boss and the lawman.

'We was doin' fine without ya, Sheriff. So you and your friend just turn your horses around and let us take care of bizness.'

Clint Mead folded his hands on his saddle horn and leaned forward.

'As I recollect, your name is Vern Kelso.'

'That's right.' Kelso's grip on his rifle tightened.

'You're Herb's ramrod.' Mead spoke with a mock casualness.

'Yep.'

Clint continued the casual banter as he dismounted. Dehner and Woody remained on their horses, watching the sheriff carefully as he stepped toward the ramrod.

'That's a fine-lookin' weapon ya got there, Vern.'

'Ah . . . thanks. . . .'

'The rifle looks new; did your momma give it to ya for your birthday?'

'Whatta ya mean?'

The lawman stopped only a few feet away from Vern Kelso.

'I mean I need to catch up on some things I owe ya.'

'Owe me?' Kelso looked confused.

'Ya do a lot of hoorawin' in town, Vern. Too much. Ya broke a few windows and knocked out some teeth. I tol' ya to start actin' smart but ya never got the message.'

Vern gave a laugh intended to impress Brawley and the ranch hands.

'A man's gotta have his fun.'

'Time for me ta have some fun.' Clint's arm became a fast blur as he smashed a fist into Kelso's face and snatched away the ramrod's rifle.

Dehner had drawn his Colt when Clint Mead attacked the

ramrod, but the action wasn't needed. Nobody tried to help Kelso. Herb Brawley and the hands broke out laughing when Kelso hit the ground, popping up dust.

The lawman spoke in a pleasant voice as he handed the Sharps-Borchardt to Brawley.

'Why don't ya hang onto this? Wouldn't want Vern ta hurt hisself.'

Kelso shouted obscenities as he struggled back onto his feet. But the man's mouth was bleeding and the muffled words sounded comical, bringing on more laughter. Vern bent over in pain, in a gesture apparently aimed at turning the mocking laughs into sympathy. It didn't work.

Mead ignored the ramrod and pointed to the man sitting on a horse.

'I see ya got Jake all ready for a ride into town. I'll keep him in jail till next week when the circuit judge arrives.'

Brawley's face crunched up and he gave a long sigh.

'Can't we jus' do the job here? The law can be pretty soft these days, Clint. I'm afraid he'll only get a jail sentence.'

'Ya got nothin' to worry 'bout.' The sheriff shook his head. 'Judge Ferguson loved that Morgan almost as much as you.'

'You're right about that,' Brawley agreed. 'Ferguson tried to buy the Morgan from me ever' time he came to town. Yep, Jake's gonna hang all right.'

'And this way the whole town will get to see it.' Clint continued to encourage the ranch owner. 'It'll be real humiliatin' – jus' what the horse thief has comin'.'

'OK, take him into town.' Herb nodded toward the horse Jake was on. 'I'll be in Candler this Saturday and pick up the chestnut then.' The ranch owner gave a quick wave to his rannies.

'Let's get back. Vern, you might wanna stop at the well and put some water on that mouth of yours – but make it quick, we gotta lot of work to get done.'

'Mr Brawley,' Woody shouted at his boss, 'can I ride into town with Jake? I mean, he's my brother and all. . . .'

'I'll leave it to you,' Herb replied as he mounted a clay-bank. 'But you'll only get paid for the hours you work. Come back now, and the cook will still have some chow left from breakfast. If you grab a bite and then go to work, I'll pay you for the whole day. Can't blame you for gettin' the law. Jake's a no-good polecat, but he's your brother.'

Woody paused for a few moments, carefully considering what he had just been told.

'Well, I am pretty hungry. . . .'

Dehner and the sheriff were the only two men riding back with the prisoner. Jake cried softly for part of the trip but his cries became louder and more anguished as they got nearer to town.

'Stop your blubberin'!' Mead snapped at the young man. 'Enjoy the sunshine. Ya won't be seein' much more of it.'

'But just ask my brother, Sheriff – he'll tell you. I ain't really a bad man.' Jake's voice was high-pitched and squeaky.

'Ya may not be bad but ya sure are stupid.' Mead wasn't impressed. 'Now shut up, you're givin' me a headache.'

CHAPTER EIGHTEEN

'How many times a week do you practice your draw, Mr Deputy Logan?'

Boone Logan smiled nervously at the nine-year-old boy, who was looking up at him with great admiration in his brown eyes.

'Well, Barry, I. . . .'

'Come along, son, Deputy Logan is busy and we need to get inside to see your father.'

Margaret Dawson placed a hand on her son's shoulder and guided him into the stage depot. Her other hand held a basket of food for her husband, Peter, who was in charge of the depot.

Boone Logan had to endure frequent taunts. *That tin star means nothin' to me* and similar jabs were shouted at him daily. Barry's hero worship provided a welcome change. Still, the deputy was glad Margaret had shooed the lad away. He didn't want to lie to the boy but he didn't want to be honest with him, either. In truth, he never practiced his draw.

Maybe I should, Logan whispered to himself. *Maybe it'd help me get ahead in this game.*

Boone Logan was fulfilling what he regarded as a humiliating duty: meeting the stage to make sure all newcomers had a good reason to be in town. He continued to whisper to himself:

Old man Candler demands that one of us be here to meet the stage if it comes in on time; he's probably lookin' out the window of the bank right now to make sure one of us is here.

'Enjoy it while you can, Mr Mayor,' he said out loud, 'you ain't gonna be holdin' office much longer.'

Boone turned around and glanced through the depot's front window to check the large clock on the wall behind the counter: almost ten minutes past 1 p.m. He returned the wave Barry gave him. The boy sat at a desk, eating lunch with his ma and pa. The deputy then strolled back to his position near a post at the end of the boardwalk. In another five minutes or so he'd be able to leave. After that, it would be a matter of possibly checking out the stage whenever it came in. Even His Honour conceded that keeping an eye out for a stage that could be hours late was, on some days, an impossible task. Still, the task was his if the sheriff and Dehner didn't get back soon.

Those thoughts moved the deputy's mind in another direction. Dehner had mentioned a US marshal who was trying to capture some owlhoots who were selling guns across the border in Mexico. Now, *that* was important work. The kind of job he was fit for. Maybe Dehner could put him in touch with that marshal, his name was . . . ?'

A familiar cacophony of pounding and rattling shattered the deputy's thoughts. The stage was arriving pretty much on time. Boone stepped back toward the depot to avoid the inevitable dust clouds.

'Howdy, Boone!' Tim Rudd's voice resounded with amusement the moment the stagecoach was at a full stop. The driver knew how much Boone hated to meet the stage.

'Howdy Tim, Ralph.'

Ralph, who was riding shotgun, smirked as he gave the deputy a two-finger salute.

'Where's Clint?' he asked.

'Out at the Brawley ranch, tryin' to stop Herb from

stringin' up some jasper who's probably got it comin'.'

Both the jehu and the shotgun chuckled as they climbed off the Concord. There were only two passengers on the stage. One was a well-dressed overweight man who was obviously a drummer. After stumbling out of the coach the salesman immediately grabbed Boone's right hand and began a spiel on the importance of dressing well.

'A man like you is already getting a lot of interested looks from the young ladies in town, no doubt about that. And a new suit can . . . .'

Boone glanced over the drummer's shoulder at the other passenger who was now looking over the town from the boardwalk. The man was not young but far from being old: probably somewhere in his late thirties. His hair was the colour of straw and his sunburned face reflected raw anger. Boone reckoned the Peacemaker tied low on the stranger's hip was rarely used to bring about peace.

Boone Logan needed to get rid of the drummer. He cut into the salesman's pitch.

'Do you sell children's clothes?'

The drummer looked surprised but didn't hesitate with his response.

'I certainly do, the very best. . . .'

'Those folks inside are hankerin' to buy some new duds for that little boy of theirs. Ya need to get inside and—'

'I will do exactly that, thank you, sir.' The drummer stepped quickly toward the back of the Concord where Tim was pulling out luggage from the boot.

Boone walked casually toward the blond-haired newcomer.

'Howdy.'

The stranger spit tobacco in the direction of the stage and said nothing. The deputy's voice became more firm.

'You in town lookin' for work?'

'Nunna your business.' The stranger faced the lawman

with milky, bloodshot eyes.

Ralph walked between Boone and the stranger, carrying a suitcase that probably belonged to the drummer. Ralph didn't notice the tension between the two men. The drummer followed behind Ralph with his sample case in hand and a toothy smile on his face.

Boone Logan followed the newcomer as he walked purposefully toward the boot. Both men stepped off the boardwalk. Tim smiled mechanically as he handed the blond man a Winchester, then he looked back at the boot.

'Guess that's all you brung with you, mister.'

Without warning, the stranger slammed the butt of the rifle into Boone's midriff. A red curtain draped over the deputy's eyes and breath exploded from his body as he crumbled to the ground.

'Stop—'

The stranger whirled the Winchester against the jehu's head before he could say anything more. Tim went into a fast spiral that ended in the dirt.

Boone managed to hold onto his consciousness. As the red curtain receded he could see the newcomer standing over him, lifting the rifle for another assault.

'Barry!' A woman's scream pierced the air as the boy ran from the office and tackled the assailant. The blond man staggered back two steps, prepared to hit the boy, but then saw two men coming at him from the direction of the office.

With Barry now clinging to one of his legs, the assailant quickly swung the rifle, hitting Ralph and Peter, the boy's father. Peter went down but Ralph stayed on his feet, though he had to cling to a nearby post.

Barry snatched the stranger's Winchester and ran with it back into the depot. The thug quickly assessed his odds. The shotgun, Ralph, was now bent over and vomiting. The deputy was struggling to his feet. Both men were armed and would soon be back in action. The stagecoach driver was regaining consciousness. The kid's mother came weeping out of the office, her son running in front of her. The drummer stood inside the depot watching through the window as he held the Winchester.

The stranger realized he'd have to kill them all to avoid prison; not much chance of that.

He ran.

Boone inhaled deeply and checked the ground. No blood was splattered around him. The blow to his stomach had almost knocked him out but hadn't seriously hurt him.

The others weren't so lucky. Boone staggered over to where Margaret was on her knees beside her husband; one arm was draped around her son. The deputy placed a hand on the boy's shoulder.

'Thanks, Barry. Ya were a real help to me.'

The boy didn't seem to hear him. He was staring with wide, terrified eyes at his father who lay on the ground a few feet from him, red liquid pooling around his head.

Ralph hurried to the depot manager and crouched over him.

'We need to get Doc Reggie, quick!' he shouted, then scooted over to where the stagecoach driver was sitting up.

'Can you handle this, Ralph?' Boone shouted. 'I'm goin' after that owlhoot.'

'Go, Boone. We'll do fine!' The command came from the wavering, squeaky voice of Tim Rudd, the jehu, on the ground.

Boone Logan's sight had now completely returned. He looked around the street in both directions. A few citizens were looking curiously in his direction. He recognized Reverend Hobart who, having heard the commotion, was running toward the depot. Good, the preacher could be of real help.

But where had the dangerous assailant gone? The young lawman tried to think like an outlaw. No sense in trying to figure out why the stranger had attacked for no reason, but what would he be doing now?

All the deputy had were some hunches; he needed to start following them up quick.

Clarence Bushrod was hunched over his store's counter while doodling on a piece of paper. He'd been trying to think up new slogans for Bernard Candler's campaign.

'If the town keeps Bernie in office there won't be no need to change the name on any of Candler's official documents,' he said to his brother, who was dusting the shelves across from him. 'Think we could come up with a snappy sayin' for that?'

'Can't think of anythin' off hand; besides, how many official documents has this town got?'

'Good point.' Clarence doodled a bit more. 'How 'bout somethin' more general, like, "Bernie is Our Boy"?'

'Nah. Mr Candler hates to be called Bernie. Ya need somethin' that plays up the man's abilities. He's ornery but he does what's best for folks – most of the time, anyhow.'

Clarence lifted his pencil high into the air. Standing behind the counter he appeared to be an orator at a town hall meeting.

'I got it, "Bernard Ain't Really So Bad".'

Rupert stopped his half-hearted dusting and faced his brother thoughtfully.

'You're gettin' there, but we need somethin' a little more upliftin'.' His face suddenly brightened as if slapped by inspiration. ' "Candler Can Do It!" '

Clarence looked confused. 'Candler can do what?'

'Ya gotta understand politiks, brother,' Rupert explained. 'Ya don't wanna get too specific – jus' say he can do it; let folks imagine the rest for themselves.'

A stranger, pistol in hand, ran into the store.

'I need a rifle and ammunition *now*!'

Clarence greeted the newcomer with a wide smile. 'You must be new in town. Most of the locals use Brighton's Mercantile across the street.'

'My brother's right,' Rupert chimed in. 'At Brighton's you'll get your rifle and ammo a lot cheaper. Tell them the Bushrod brothers sent ya, they might give ya a discount.'

The stranger did a half turn and waved his gun between the two brothers.

'You'll both do like I tell ya. Get me a rifle and ammo and show me a place where I can hide out.'

'Sorry, friend,' Clarence threw his arms up in a gesture of resignation, 'but ya see my brother and me is tied up in a political race right now. If we were caught harboring a gunman, well, it would sink our candidate's chances, and the election is this Saturday.'

'Sorry, but it's true what they say, politiks turns people against each other.' Rupert's voice struck a chord of sadness.

The gunman stepped behind Rupert, clamped an arm around his neck and pressed a gun against the side of the storekeeper's head. A vicious desperation laced the stranger's voice as he looked at Clarence.

'I ain't got time to listen to a lotta jabberin'. You're gonna do what I say or your brother dies.'

Clarence once again threw up his arms, this time in a gesture of joy.

'Hallelujah!'

'What the—?' Fear of his captives' weirdness cut into the gunman's desperation.

'Last Sunday morning my brother and me went to church and got ourselves saved,' Clarence explained. 'We know that when we leave this mortal coil of strife and suffering we are going to a better place that the Lord has prepared for us.'

'Clarence is right, jus' take a look around.' With the gunman's arm pressing against his windpipe Rupert's voice was more high-pitched than usual but he still sounded cheerful. 'Preparin' us a better place than the Bushrod brothers' general store probably won't demand much of the Lord.'

The brothers were banking on the assumption that their captor had a less than great intellect. Their assumption was correct. The gunman's eyes darted nervously between the brothers and the front window. He paid no heed to the back door. Boone Logan, having heard Clarence and Rupert's loud voices, had crept in through the back and was now only a few feet away from the gunman.

'Once ya put a bullet in my brother's brain, what there is of it, why don't ya shoot me?' Clarence suggested. 'That way the Bushrod brothers can enter the pearly gates together. What a glorious—'

Boone grabbed the stranger's gun hand and twisted it. As the pistol dropped to the floor, Boone moved his right foot to step on it. That was a mistake. The stranger pushed Rupert into the deputy. Boone and Rupert toppled over together in a tangle of arms and legs.

Rupert's foot collided with the pistol, sending it on a fast skid toward the back of the store. The stranger went running after it.

'Grab the gun under the counter,' Rupert shouted to his brother.

'There ain't no gun under the counter,' Clarence shouted back.

'Oh. . . .' Rupert's tone turned apologetic. 'Always intended to put one there. . . .'

Boone had freed himself from Rupert, though he was still lying on the floor when he drew his Colt.

'Stop where ya are, mister,' he ordered the stranger. 'Stay away from the gun.'

The order went unheeded. The stranger quickly scooped up the weapon – but he was not quick enough. A hot flame from Boone's Colt speared into his shoulder; the gunman's body jerked violently. He staggered backwards, tripped on a broom Rupert had left lying on the floor and flopped onto the boards.

Boone ran to the fallen outlaw, slammed a foot onto his wrist and grabbed the six-shooter from his hand. The gunman continued to bellow in pain as Rupert hurried to the deputy's side.

'The man is bleedin',' he said. 'We gotta get him to the doc quick. Those bloodstains will never come outta the floor.'

Clarence left the counter and joined the group. 'This would happen right after we got around to sweeping the floor.' He looked at his brother. 'The Good Book is right: "*Vanity, vanity, all is vanity*". Yep, vanity is useless.'

'What's that got to do with anythin'? Rupert asked. 'Vanity means pride.'

'Oh,' Clarence replied. 'I thought it meant hard work. Thanks for settin' me straight.'

'You learn somethin' new ever' day.' Rupert smiled approvingly.

The gunman continued to holler in pain.

Boone Logan joined the outlaw's victims who were now comfortably seated on the two large sofas in Doc Reggie's waiting area. The doctor was attending to the wounded thug. Young Barry wanted to hear all the details of how Boone had shot down the dangerous bad man. With his father now safe and sitting beside him drinking a glass of water, Barry was once again seeking sensational diversion.

Logan gave the boy a subdued but accurate account of what had happened in the Bushrod brothers' general store while Margaret fussed over the bandage on her husband's head.

'Barry, leave the deputy alone,' she admonished. 'I'm sure he has important matters to attend to.' The woman gave

Boone an accusatory stare.

A table on which stood a large pitcher of water was set in front of two sofas that formed an L in the waiting area. Doc Reggie had ordered Peter, Tim and Ralph to sit for a while and drink plenty of water before leaving. Like Peter, the jehu and the shotgun had bandaged heads. Ralph refilled a glass from the pitcher as he gave Boone a lopsided smile.

'Did you find any identification on that owlhoot?' he asked.

Logan shook his head. 'All he had in his pockets was a couple of coins.'

Tim took a large gulp of water. 'Were you able to question him?' Again, the deputy shook his head.

'The doc gave him laudanum. That jasper won't be talkin' much till tomorrow morning.'

Boone stood up and smiled at his companions. 'Glad to see none of ya was hurt too bad. I've run Clarence and Rupert outta here like the doctor asked, guess that's 'bout all I can do to help him. I gotta get back to the office. See ya all later.'

As he passed the hotel Boone noticed that Dehner's bay was tied up in front of it. Apparently the troubles at the Brawley ranch had been taken care of. The deputy prepared himself to explain to his boss exactly what had happened in his absence, but as he entered the office he was surprised to see Clint Mead talking with a well-dressed gent.

What now? he thought to himself.

CHAPTER NINETEEN

Rance Dehner had left the hotel and started to walk toward the sheriff's office when he spotted Boone Logan running toward him. The deputy was wheezing as he stopped in front of the detective.

'Sheriff Mead wants ya over at Doc Reggie's.'

'Sure, but why?' Dehner paused and changed the direction of his steps.

As they walked toward the doctor's house Boone explained what had happened while Dehner and the sheriff were preoccupied with preventing a hanging. Dehner remained confused.

'But why does Clint want me over at the doc's house?'

' 'Bout the time you and the sheriff got back to Candler, a man arrived from the railroad. He's a detective, sorta like you, but he sure does dress a lot better – if ya don't mind my sayin' so. His name is Brad Cody.'

'So . . . this Brad Cody is a railroad detective employed by the Union West Railroad?'

'Yep. He's here investigatin' the disappearance of Stephen Montague, the railroad man who spoke up for Enoch at that political rally last Saturday. When he heard 'bout the jasper I shot, he wanted to see him right away. Don't know why. The sheriff don't know either but he thought you'd wanna be there.'

The two men, now within sight of Doc Reggie's home, spotted the sheriff and a companion coming out of it. Mead and the man with him waited until the deputy and Rance were in speaking range. The sheriff made a quick introduction as the four men stood in front of the doctor's house.

'Rance Dehner, this here is Brad Cody, a detective with the Union . . . .'

As Mead spoke Dehner mused to himself that Brad Cody was, indeed, very well dressed. His clothes were similar to those of Bernard Candler: a brown suit and derby. But Cody's suit was newer and more impressive than the banker's faded duds.

Their clothes showed the only similarity between Cody and Bernard Candler. Brad Cody was a large, raw-boned man in his early forties. His face was still handsome despite pock marks, probably from a childhood disease, and two front teeth were lacking, probably due to a fight.

'Stephen Montague has gone missing,' Clint Mead said. 'Mr Cody here believes that the man Boone shot today knows something about it.'

'How do you figure that, Mr Cody?' Dehner looked questioningly at Cody. Cody gave a brief smile.

'Please gents, call me Brad. I like things on a first-name basis.'

There were polite nods all around, then Brad Cody continued: 'The man lying inside is Stephen Montague's brother, Lewis.'

Boone Logan pushed his hat back and shook his head. 'I shoulda thought of that; both men have blond hair that looks—'

'Forget it, Boone, you ain't the first man not to connect Lewis and Stephen Montague,' Cody assured the deputy. 'In many ways, they're as different as two men can be. Stephen is hard-working, a man you can trust. Lewis is a no-account: a thief and a gunman and not very good at doing either. Still,

Stephen cared about his brother; you could say the two were close.'

'Why does Lewis think his brother is missing?' Dehner asked.

'Stephen and Lewis both live in Griswold, not far from here. In truth, Stephen don't spend much time there anymore, too busy travelling around on business. But after he left Candler last Saturday, Stephen was heading home to take a few days off and do some fishing with his brother.'

'And he never showed,' Sheriff Mead added.

'Before he left Griswold,' the railroad detective continued, 'Lewis telegraphed us that he was coming here to look into things.'

'He didn't say nothin' 'bout that when he got off the stage.' Logan's face crunched up as he cupped a hand over his jaw. 'He didn't say much of anythin', jus' started actin' crazy.'

'Lewis *is* a bit crazy,' Cody responded. 'I've done some fishing with the brothers. Lewis likes to drink – yep – he likes it a lot. He's downed a lot of rotgut. I think the stuff has battered his brain.'

'What do you think Lewis hoped to find in Candler regarding his brother?' Rance asked.

Cody inhaled deeply before answering:

'Stephen has been talking to folks at our company about some strange goings-on regarding the railroad coming into Candler, but he was never specific. I'm hoping he might have been more open in talking with his brother. Once we find out about all that, well, maybe we'll be closer to discovering what happened to Stephen.'

Dehner glanced at the doctor's house, then asked another question:

'When can we talk to Lewis?'

'That won't be 'till tomorrow morning.' The sheriff gave a whimsical laugh. 'Doc Reggie has given the man laudanum and don't want anybody jawin' to Lewis till he's had a good night's sleep to recover. The doc's feelin' a bit ornery right now; can't blame him, he's had a pretty busy day.'

'Guess we've all had a pretty busy day,' Clint Mead said, looking at the sky. 'Why don't we tie on the feed bag?'

'Sounds good to me!' Cody exclaimed. Boone's eyes brightened.

'Say, Mr Cody, do ya suppose ya could call this a business supper and have the Union West Railroad pay for the vittles?'

Brad Cody said nothing.

A man looked up at the dark night sky and smiled: no moon and no stars. The only light came from the lanterns hanging in front of the Prairie Dog saloon, which stood at a safe distance away. The man continued to muse on his good luck as he approached the house of Doctor Reginald Dalrymple. The doctor was off somewhere, delivering a baby.

Not a board squeaked as the man stepped onto the porch. He could move soundlessly: it was one of the skills a man in his profession had to hone. Contemptuous thoughts of past associates bungling a job by a careless misstep or colliding with a piece of furniture they should have known was there streaked through the killer's mind.

Those fools deserved jail or a coffin. Not he. He wasn't stupid. He was a man who knew the lay of the land. Doc Reggie always left his house unlocked when he went to visit a patient. That way any sick folks who came to see him while he was gone could lie down on one of his sofas until the doc returned.

He opened the door, but only a quarter of the way. Somewhere near being half-opened and the damn thing would have begun to squeak. The killer slipped inside and cautiously closed the door.

He paused for a moment and collected his thoughts. Every job came with uncertainties and he needed to be ready for them. The killer crept with panther-like motion toward the two sofas arranged in an L-shape. No one was there. Good. If no one came, there would only need to be one killing tonight.

The other uncertainty bothered him more. Laudanum was strong stuff but it affected people in different ways. The jasper waiting for him inside the doc's surgery could either be in a drug-induced deep sleep or awake, gritting his teeth in pain and wondering when the doc would get back.

Whichever, there was a job to be done here.

The door to the surgery was quieter than the front door. Still, the killer opened it only to the degree that was necessary for him to slip inside. He then became as a statue, allowing his eyes to adjust to the more intense darkness of the surgery.

There was one large window in the room but the doctor always kept the shade pulled down. Some light came from the shade's two sides: not much light but it was all he needed.

The killer listened carefully for any indication of consciousness from his prey. There were no sounds of rustling or speech. If the jasper was awake he was unaware of a visitor.

The killer's movements could have been called graceful as he slithered across the room and stood over the blond-haired victim. The wounded man's eyes opened slightly; they were drowsy from the laudanum.

The drowsiness vanished and the eyes became bigger as they saw a hooded figure hovering above. The victim tried to yell but it was too late. A hand was firmly clamped over his mouth. The blond-haired man could only watch in terror as a large knife came down and plunged into his heart.

The killer's steps remained cautious and graceful as he moved away, content with his work. On leaving the house he once again opened the door only a quarter of the way. He didn't want to make the slightest squeak.

CHAPTER TWENTY

'Rance, you're OK. I was afraid those terrible men had killed you.'

The young woman ran to Rance Dehner and embraced him.

Dehner looked into Beth Page's blue eyes and realized she was the only woman he wanted to share his life with.

'I'm fine, Beth, and now we have a whole lifetime to spend together.'

That statement seemed to confuse the girl. 'I don't think so, I don't think so.'

She took a step back from him.

'Come back, Beth, please!'

The girl began to cry. 'I pleaded with you not to go into that saloon after those outlaws. You were only a deputy. The sheriff would have been back soon.'

'I didn't know that! The sheriff could have been gone for most of the day.'

Dehner's voice became defensive, he sounded like a man pleading his case before a judge. 'Those thugs had already beaten up one of the saloon girls. I had to act. Why did you have to run into the saloon, Beth? I told you—'

'There were shots, you collapsed,' she yelled back at him.

'I dropped to the floor, to become a harder target. . . .'

'You saw me standing outside the saloon. You should have

stopped and taken me away before the gunplay. But you were too proud.'

'I'm sorry, Beth, please. I didn't know a bullet would find you.'

Blood suddenly covered the girl's body.

'I love you, Beth.' Rance shouted the words but darkness began to enfold the bleeding girl and he felt she couldn't hear him. If he could only move. . . .

Dehner's eyes opened and, for a moment, he didn't know where he was. *Another hotel room in another town . . . yes . . . this is Candler.*

The detective had no desire to return to sleep. He was all too conscious of what could be waiting for him there. He lit the bedside lamp, got out of bed and dressed.

When Rance had all of his clothes on, except his boots, he parted the curtains on the room's one window and looked out on the town, now dimly visible under a gray sky. The detective tried to think about the circumstances that had brought him to Candler, but he couldn't manage it, not yet.

What would his life have been like if Beth Page had lived? That was a question Dehner knew would torture him for the rest of his life. It all seemed so long ago, and yet it also seemed like yesterday. He had been sixteen when he made that tragic mistake. He should have stopped dealing with a gang of hardcases in a saloon when he saw Beth watching from outside, her face clearly visible over the batwings. He should have taken her home right then, but he didn't want to look like he was backing down. When the shooting started he had hit the ground; Beth misunderstood. She ran in and. . . .

Dehner closed his eyes. *Will I ever stop reliving that day?*

He knew the answer to that question.

Beth had been fourteen when she died. A sad, whimsical smile came to Dehner's face: *Or fourteen and a half,* as she had always insisted on saying. He paused and looked toward the sky.

'I think of you every day, Beth,' he murmured. There was no reply. There never was.

Would he ever find peace, or what the Good Book called redemption? That was another question for which he already knew the answer. But Dehner knew he had to keep trying. He recalled his earlier musings and realized he could never settle into the life of a rancher or storekeeper; he must try and make amends. . . .

The detective made a fist and slammed it against the hotel wall. A lot of good he was doing the troubled folks of Candler, including a five-year-old child who, he felt, was in immediate danger. He needed to stop agonizing over the past and get busy trying to resolve the terrors of today.

The detective's mind raced over everything that had happened since he first saw Jenny Scott step out from a grove of trees. Patches of facts and theories scrambled about in his mind but he couldn't quite bring them together into a pattern.

Maybe breakfast would help; the café nearby opened earlier than the hotel restaurant. They would at least have some coffee ready. He smiled inwardly. It would certainly beat Boone Logan's coffee.

Dehner left his second-floor room, waved at the desk clerk as he hit the bottom of the stairway and made his way out the front door. He began to cross the street but stopped not far past the hitch rail as he spotted Doc Reggie's coat tails flapping about. The doctor was doing a fast walk toward the sheriff's office.

Dehner sighed and whispered to himself: 'Looks like I'll have to settle for Boone's coffee after all.'

CHAPTER TWENTY-ONE

Five men with grim expressions paced about the waiting area of Doctor Reginald Dalrymple's house. The two sofas remained empty.

'It was well past midnight when I delivered the Weldons' baby,' Doc Reggie explained. 'They encouraged me to sleep at their place for a few hours before riding back. I took them up on the offer. When I returned home I checked on my patient first thing and found him murdered.'

Brad Cody muttered a string of disconnected profanities before speaking in a loud voice.

'This crime is somehow connected to my company. I know it.'

'How's that?' Sheriff Mead asked.

'Stephen Montague jawed with the Union West Railroad people who had been to Candler to discuss the possibilities of the railroad coming through this town,' Cody answered. 'Something about the situation in Candler made him suspicious; that much we know.'

'What exactly was botherin' him?' The question came from Boone Logan. Rance Dehner, who stood beside the deputy, had thus far remained quiet.

'I ain't got no idea,' Cody shouted. 'Stephen was a real

cautious sort of man. He wouldn't say anything official-like that he couldn't prove. But he wouldn't be so careful when talking with his brother.'

'You think he got more to the point with his brother.' Clint Mead was clarifying a fact, not asking a question.

Brad nodded his head.

'Lewis Montague knew something real important; now it's going to be buried with him.' Cody sighed deeply, looked at the floor and then spoke to Dehner. 'I unnerstand that outfit you work for, the Lowrie Agency, has sent you on some rail-road business.'

'That's right.'

'Ever do anything for Union West?'

'No.'

Cody again looked down at the floor.

'All the railroads is pretty much the same,' he opined. 'They're run by hard men who don't let nothing get in their way. They expect results and they expect 'em yesterday.' He raised his head and looked around at all of the men in the room. 'I'll be honest, gents: finding out what happened to Stephen is important to me and it ain't just because he's a fellow railroad man. My job may be on the line. Any help you can give me will sure be appreciated.'

'The only help I can give right now is to get the body to the undertaker's,' Doc Reggie responded. 'That is, unless you gentlemen want to examine the corpse again.'

The doctor received negative looks all around. Clint Mead was the first to speak.

'Seems I'm the one who's always thinkin' about his stomach, but after the doc does what's he's gotta do why don't we all get over to the café and have ourselves some breakfast? Things might look a little better then.'

The five men had breakfast together but things didn't look any better afterwards. The men still appeared grim when they left the café and went their separate ways.

Dehner accompanied Clint and his deputy to the sheriff's office, where matters did brighten up. Sylvia Kaplan stood by the front door with a small, wide box in her hand and a large jar of candy.

'Ah, mornin' Sylvia.' Mead sounded nervous as he unlocked the office door. His entire body became fidgety as he entered the office behind everyone else.

The young woman didn't notice the lawman's unease. Her spirits were obviously high as she placed her items on the sheriff's desk.

'Enoch and I really appreciate you helping us out, Sheriff. I managed to get about half of these things done last night, but what with keeping an eye on Jenny and—'

'I don't mind at all, don't mind at—'

'I've got the tags on the tobacco pouches.' Sylvia motioned at the box. 'All you have to do is spoon in the candy and tie them up. Oh, there's also string and a spoon in the box.'

'Thanks – ah – thanks.' Trying to sound official the sheriff asked: 'How is Jenny doin'?'

The young woman's face brightened. 'She's improving every day. She talks more and more, but so far she only talks about Goliath. I'm hoping and praying that in another few weeks, she'll be talking in a normal manner.'

'Maybe she'll tell us what happened when her parents got killed,' Boone Logan blurted out.

'I wouldn't depend on that, Deputy.' Sylvia's countenance became more somber. 'I'd be very hesitant to ask Jenny about what happened on that terrible day. It might cause her to take another retreat into silence.'

Sylvia paused, then thanked the sheriff again for his help and left with polite goodbyes to Dehner and Logan. As soon as she had left the deputy slammed a fist into the palm of his left hand.

'Will I ever stop sayin' the wrong things around women?'

'Probably not,' the sheriff answered.

Dehner changed the subject. 'Looks like you're doing some political work today.' He nodded toward the objects recently placed on the sheriff's desk.

'Yep.' Clint Mead looked down in embarrassment. 'I reckon I owe this to Enoch.'

'Why's that?' Boone's eyes grew bigger as he focused on the jar of candy.

Clint ran a hand through his hair in a gesture of frustration.

'Well, as you gents probably already figgered out, I was sorta behind that political debate last Saturday.'

Dehner gave the sheriff a crooked smile. 'Bernard Candler isn't much of a talker. You thought Enoch would easily carry the day, especially with a railroad representative there to speak for him.'

'That's what I reckoned,' Mead's frustration began to edge its way into anger. 'but the Bushrod brothers sorta walked away with it. All most folks remember about the debate is that the Bushrods were funny and Bernard gave away free candy.'

Boone began to laugh and couldn't stifle the guffaw even when his boss gave him an angry stare.

'So now you're copyin' the Bushrods' notion.' The deputy gestured toward the jar of candy.

Clint Mead sighed and nodded his head.

'Yep. Enoch and me is plannin' on holdin' a little political rally tomorrow night after the prayer meeting. Won't be the same as a Saturday affair but the election is this Saturday, so we'll just do what we can.'

The idea could work out well, Dehner silently acknowledged. Wednesday-night prayer meetings were common in the West and served as a social as well as a religious function. Ranching could be an isolating experience. People liked to come into town at mid-week to reconnect with each other. As

Clint noted, the crowd wouldn't be as big as on Saturday but there would be quite a few folks there.

Boone looked unconvinced of the wisdom of this move.

'What if the Bushrods show up and start tellin' jokes and. . . .'

'They can't do that,' the sheriff told him. 'This is a political rally, not a debate.'

'But that ain't the way things is supposed to work.' Boone still looked unconvinced. 'Ever' candidate for office should get his say, that's what freedom—'

'If Bernard Candler wants to hold a political rally, he has the freedom to do so,' Sheriff Mead replied, shouting.

'I see . . . I guess.' The deputy looked sheepish, then his eyes brightened. 'Say, I'm gonna vote for Enoch; do you reckon I could have a bit of that candy right now?'

'No!' The sheriff's voice once again boomed at his deputy.

Dehner immediately suggested to Boone that they do a round together. Deputy Logan responded with a quick nod of agreement. The morning round consisted primarily of rousting sleeping drunks from their place of slumber: the back of the Bushrod brothers' general store. The process was slow and unpleasant. The revelers from the previous night were now tired and headachy. Some of them had trouble getting to their feet. All of them were in a persnickety frame of mind.

Boone Logan asked Rance to do the regular check on the bank.

'Bernard knows the sheriff and me is supportin' Enoch in the election. I'd jus' as soon not have the old goat glarin' at me.'

As Dehner entered the bank two tellers were setting up for the day. The detective walked to the open door of Bernard Candler's office.

'Good morning, Mr Candler.'

'Good morning . . . Mr Dehner, is it?'

'Yes, I'm a volunteer deputy.'

'I know what you are, Mr Dehner; thanks for looking in on us.'

Rance exited the bank believing the bank president was handling his perilous political situation fairly well. He was a lot more cordial than the crowd behind the Bushrod brothers' general store.

Bernard Candler's reasonably good temper may have been boosted later on by the fact that both deputies were on hand to meet the stagecoach, which arrived early at a few minutes before 1 p.m. Boone Logan's mood was further uplifted when he saw that the stage had no passengers and thus there was no reason to inform newcomers of the town's unofficial rule regarding employment.

The fragile good nature of the day was shattered when the two deputies returned to the sheriff's office after doing their duty in regard to the stage. Sheriff Mead was spooning candy into small brown pouches.

'Ain't ya got that done yet?' Logan shouted.

'I ain't had the chance,' Clint Mead shouted back. 'Most o' the mornin' got took up with all the fool paperwork the government makes me do. Then there was the folks who walked in wantin' this or that. They laughed when they saw the jar of candy. Like there was somethin' dern funny 'bout a jar of candy.'

Logan beamed a wide smile. 'What they thought was funny is you copyin' an idea from the Bushrod brothers instead of thinkin' up an idea of your own.' He spoke in the manner of one imparting great wisdom.

'I know all that, Mr Smarty Pants.' Mead threw the spoon onto his desk and glared at the deputy.

Dehner felt relieved when he heard frantic footsteps running toward the sheriff's office, though it was obvious that whoever was coming was bringing bad news.

The front door flew open and a boy of about eight came

running in. His hair was dark and his cheeks were hollowed by malnutrition. His clothes were dirty and spotted with holes. The soles on his shoes were thin and loose. His voice was high pitched and panicky.

'Sheriff, ya gotta come quick, right now.'

The anger on Sheriff Mead's face vanished, to be replaced by concern.

'Now, calm down, Jamie.' He stepped from behind his desk and placed his hands on the boy's shoulders. 'Take a deep breath and tell me what's happened.'

Jamie inhaled and paused for a moment. His voice still rang with urgency when he spoke.

'Pa's terrible mad, he's gonna kill Slade.'

Clint gave the boy a kind smile. 'Jamie, you know your pa gets in a bad temper now and then and threatens to do things he never does.'

'This time he really means it.' The boy's face contorted and tears trailed down both cheeks. 'Ma tole me to tell ya Pa is really actin' crazy. She woulda come herself but Polly's gettin' kinda heavy to carry . . . she's three . . . Ma knew I could get here faster.'

'Tell me exactly what your pa has done.' Mead's voice remained a steady monotone.

'You know that bluff near our place?' the boy asked.

'Yes.' The sheriff nodded his head. 'Both Boone and I have been out there.'

'Well, Pa has Slade holed up at the top of the bluff. He's at the bottom with a rifle. He's waitin' him out. Pa says Slade will starve at the top of the bluff or he's gonna kill him when he tries to come down, whichever – makes no never mind to Pa, Slade is gonna end up dead.'

'Why does your pa wanna kill Slade?' This time the sheriff's voice wasn't quite so steady.

'Don't know,' Jamie answered. 'I asked Ma and she tol' me now's not the time to jaw about that. You gotta ride out to our place, *now*!'

The sheriff squeezed Jamie's shoulders, then looked at his two deputies.

'This might . . . could be serious. Could ya ride out to the Hollister place?'

'No, Sheriff, you should come. I'll ride with ya.'

Clint spoke in a reassuring manner to the boy: 'I'm sending the two best deputies in Arizona out to your place. They can handle anythin'. I'll bet ya rode hard comin' into Candler.'

'Yep.'

'We'll take your horse to the livery, get him a rub-down and some oats.' The sheriff looked at the boy in a knowing manner: two men of the world discussing important matters. 'The horse will need to rest before ya start back. So, ya can help me with my sheriff duties for a few hours.'

Jamie's emotions were at high speed and he needed a moment to process what he had just been told.

'Well . . . OK.'

The sheriff let go of the boy and stood to his full height.

'Before we get started, would you like a few gumdrops?'

Jamie nodded his head. The sheriff opened the candy jar and motioned with his free hand for his deputies to get riding.

'Who is the boy's father, and who's Slade?' Dehner asked as the two men hit the boardwalk outside the office.

'Jamie's pa is Levi Hollister. Slade is Jamie's half-brother. Levi's first wife died a long ways back. Levi remarried some gal named Dotty. Dotty don't come inta town much.'

Boone had answered the detective's questions while the two men untied their horses from the hitch rail in front of the sheriff's office. They mounted and set their steeds moving at a steady gait down the town's main street.

'Why would Levi want to kill his own son?' Dehner was keeping his bay a step or two behind Boone's cayuse. The

116

deputy knew where they were going.

'The Lord only knows,' Logan answered. 'Maybe I should say the Devil only knows. Both Levi and Slade are no-accounts, gettin' drunk is the only thing they're good at. You seen how Jamie looks. The whole family is half-starved, only Slade ain't like Jamie, he's growed up. Levi and Slade are both violent men. No tellin' what will happen if they start fightin' each other.'

They were now near the edge of town. Both men spurred their horses into a strong gallop.

CHAPTER TWENTY-TWO

As the two men neared the Hollister place Rance could smell a heavy, repulsive sweetness in the air. They pulled up near a dilapidated structure. Pieces of broken jugs lay scattered over the ground.

'Are Levi and Slade moonshiners?' Dehner asked.

'They got themselves a still out back but they ain't exactly moonshiners.'

'What do you mean?'

'Levi and Slade make tanglefoot but they jus' drink it themselves, by and large,' Boone answered. 'They ain't ambitious enough to really get out and sell the stuff.'

As the two men dismounted Rance spotted a female face at the shack's one window. The face was bony, with frightened eyes and stringy hair. When the woman realized the detective had seen her she hastily stepped into the darkness of the shack.

Two shots came from about fifteen yards away, followed by angry shouts. Both men ground-tethered their horses, then ran toward a bluff on the right side of the house. The bluff was squat, spotted with stones and various ragged, sharp-leaved plants. It seemed to reflect the human poverty and desolation that lived beside it.

More shots came from the top of the bluff. Dehner and Logan took cover behind a large boulder facing the bluff. Boone raised his head only slightly above the large rock. 'Levi, you up there?' he called out.

'Yep. Not that it be any of your business, Depety.'

'Where's Slade?' Boone kept his voice a shout.

'He's right here with me. Both of us got guns and we plan on usin' 'em. We're gonna kill ever'body in that broken-down shack, and burn it to the ground. After that, we head out for Candler and do some more killin'. We might even set fire to the whole town. Why, you'll have to find another town to make ya a depety, Boone.'

Logan crouched down and looked at Dehner.

'This don't make no sense. Jamie tol' us Levi and Slade were gettin' ready to kill each other. Now they seem to be actin' together.'

The detective smirked as he looked upward. 'Never underestimate the power of a father's love for his son.'

Boone gave a joyless laugh. 'Reckon so.'

Rance looked at the ground, then eyed his companion.

'Has Levi threatened his family before?'

'Sorta,' Logan muttered. 'He bragged in a saloon a few months back 'bout beatin' his woman. The sheriff and I rode out here to check on it. Dotty had been beaten all right but she gave us a fool story 'bout fallin' down. Nothin' much we could do.'

A gunshot ended the discussion. Levi had fired his Winchester.

'You worthless lawdogs gonna leave now or do I have ta kill ya?' he shouted.

'Levi, Slade, both of ya throw out your guns, and walk down slow-like with your hands up.' Boone's reply sounded mechanical, a man observing what he knew was a pointless legal requirement.

Mocking laughter and loud curses streamed down from

the top of the bluff.

Dehner cast a curious look upward toward their adversaries.

'They've fired at us twice – neither shot came even close.'

'Yeah, well, both Hollisters probably got their guts filled with tanglefoot.'

Another wild shot pierced the air followed by a blare of muddled words from both Levi and Slade.

Dehner pulled the Colt from its holster.

'The sun is setting. This situation will get worse with nightfall,' he murmured to Boone. 'Spray some bullets at Slade and his daddy. I'll go around back and come up on them from behind.'

'That's a plenty obvious trick, don't ya think?'

'Yes,' Rance admitted, 'but we're dealing with drunken amateurs.'

Dehner bent into a jackknife posture and ran from the boulder as Boone spewed hot lead upwards. The detective believed he had not been spotted by either of the Hollisters.

But were Levi and Slade really worried by any action he took? An idea was forming in Dehner's mind as he ran in a half-circle to the other side of the bluff. He hoped his notion was wrong.

Rance advanced quietly up the bluff. Halfway up he holstered his weapon, crouched and crab-walked the rest of the way. As he reached the top of the bluff he saw Levi and Slade. The father and son were giggling to themselves as they lay flat on the ground, shouting at Boone Logan and sending off the occasional shot.

They don't look like desperate men bent on a rampage of killing and destruction, Dehner thought to himself. Their mood was playful, like two small boys telling dirty jokes in the back of the schoolroom.

The detective palmed his Colt, resumed full height and took several steps toward the Hollisters.

'Lay down your guns, both of you, and get up slowly.'

Levi and Slade turned around; their faces expressed surprise but neither man looked worried – they could barely hide their amusement. Both men were dressed in patched overalls and large floppy hats. Their eyes looked like glass and showed an odd sense of joy. Rance Dehner was the man who was becoming worried.

The detective called down to Logan as the two prisoners carried out his instructions. Dehner waited until the deputy was at the top of the bluff before he began with the questions.

'What exactly has been going on here?'

'Me and Slade got ourselves a bit crazy; sorry if we caused you gents some trouble.'

Boone's face crunched in doubt. 'Jamie tol' us you was set on killin' Slade, Levi. You sayin' that ain't true?'

Slade's face brightened, he appeared to be enjoying himself.

'Pa gets real loco sometimes and says stuff that don't count for sour apples.'

The deputy wasn't convinced. 'Jamie claimed his ma sent him, is she loco too?'

'You lawdogs know what womenfolks are like.' This time Levi answered. 'But I'll say this for Dotty, she kin make a right nice stew. Why don't you jaspers stay for some vittles? That'll sorta make up for us bringin' ya all the ways out here for nothin' much.'

Slade turned his head around and lowered his face into his hands in an unsuccessful attempt to cover his laughing. Dehner realized his suspicions were true.

The detective forced a smile onto his face and friendliness into his voice as he holstered his weapon and placed his hands on the shoulders of Levi and Slade.

'Why sure, Boone and I would be honored to chow down with two outstanding citizens like yourselves.'

121

Dehner slammed the two men together and pushed them to the ground. 'Keep a close eye on Slade, Boone.' Boone stepped a little closer.

'You're working for somebody, Levi.' Rance pressed a booted foot down on Levi's throat. 'You made your wife tell Jamie a lot of hogwash in order to get Boone and me out here and away from Candler. I want to know who put you up to it and why.'

'Don't know what you're talkin' 'bout.'

Levi's voice rasped under the boot. He wrapped bony fingers around Dehner's toe and heel and pushed, to no effect.

Dehner pressed his foot further into Levi's throat.

'I have little time and less patience. Are you going to tell me the truth or am I going to have to break one of your arms? The choice is yours, Levi.'

'OK, OK.' Levi's voice now conveyed surrender.

'Talk, and no lies.' Dehner lifted the pressure off his victim's neck, but only by a little bit.

Levi kept his hands on the boot.

'The idea was ta git Boone and the sheriff out here, not you. Least, I think that was the plan.'

Dehner glanced at the other Hollister. Slade lay on the ground, under Logan's pistol. The joy had vanished from his face, to be replaced by defeat. The detective had to admit to himself that he preferred it that way.

'OK, Levi,' Dehner continued, 'tell me how you got this notion.'

'It weren't my idea.' Levi's voice was defensive.

'Then whose idea was it?'

'That's kinda a strange story.'

'Get started with it.'

'Well, yesterday I was in town pickin' up supplies.' Levi seemed to be trying to arrange his thoughts. 'I stopped in at the Prairie Dog – jus' fer one drink, mind ya.'

'Keep on,' Dehner prodded.

'I left the Prairie Dog feelin' sick like to my stomach, so I went behind the saloon to the woods out back. I threw up my breakfast – and my lunch too, I reckon.'

'Then what happened?' Dehner said.

'Some feller pushed me to the ground, like you jus' did, only I landed on my face and could feel the barrel of a gun pressed agin my neck.'

'Did you see the man's face at all?'

'I kinda turned my head some to git a look,' Levi answered. 'But it didn't do no good.'

'Why not?' Dehner's response was crisp.

'The feller was wearin' a black hood of some kind. Looked right scary.'

'What did he say to you?'

A look of confusion came over Levi Hollister's face, as if he were still struggling to understand what had been said to him.

'The feller spoke in a nice voice, claimed he had a easy job for me, a job that'd pay good.'

'This job entailed getting Jamie to skedaddle into town with a story that would get the law to ride out to your place.' The detective grimaced as anger with himself shot through him. 'You and Slade were to get the law to stay here as long as you could.'

'That's right. Think maybe ya kin lift your foot jus' a bit more?'

Dehner obliged. 'Did this man tell you why he was willing to pay you to do this?'

'Nah. I asked him 'bout that and sudden-like his voice weren't so nice. He tol' me it was nunna my business.'

'How much did he pay you?'

'Five dollars.' A look of sadness came over the elder Hollister's face. 'Said he'd pay me another five iffen I'd did the job good. Guess I kin fergit 'bout that.'

The detective sighed and asked a question to which he already knew the answer:

'How did this fellow plan to pay you the second five dollars?'

'He didn't say, jus' said he'd do it.'

'So, you terrified Jamie and turned your wife into a liar for five dollars and the hope of another five?'

'A man's gotta make a livin'.'

Dehner looked at Boone Logan, who sensed the question in the detective's eyes.

'I'm sure he's tellin' the truth,' he said. 'Levi ain't got that much imagination.'

Dehner lifted his foot completely off Levi's neck and glanced at the darkening sky. Neither action made him feel any better. Anger and resignation laced his voice.

'Boone and I are carrying both of your rifles down to the foot of the bluff and leaving them there. You jaspers are to stay up here until you see us ride off.'

Slade appeared irritated by the orders. 'What fer?' he snapped as he and his father got back onto their feet.

'Because I'm sick of looking at both of you.' Dehner picked up the two rifles and handed one to Boone Logan. The two of them hastily trotted down the bluff, tossed the rifles away and broke into a run for their horses.

Even as they mounted both men realized they had been tricked, but there was no help for it. Logan patted his black on the neck and whispered a few curses.

'We rode these horses hard getting out here.' Dehner spoke aloud what the deputy was thinking. 'We need to ride back slow and easy, otherwise we could kill our animals.'

'Don't know what's goin' on in town right now.' Boone looked toward Candler. 'Jus' hope Sheriff Mead can handle it alone.'

CHAPTER TWENTY-THREE

Sylvia Kaplan locked the front door of Brighton's Mercantile and reversed the sign in the window, so those passing by would know the store was closed. She laughed quietly to herself. Everyone in town knew the store closed at 7 p.m. on most weeknights, except Wednesdays when it closed at five. Brighton's closed at 6 p.m. on Saturdays and was closed on Sundays. Keeping a sign in the window was hardly necessary.

The young woman giggled out loud as she made her way behind the store counter and pulled out the accounts book. She was in a very giddy mood.

Her thoughts turned to Reverend Giles Hobart. The preacher was beginning to truly fit in. He had been kind enough to rent a horse for Jamie Hollister from the livery and ride with Jamie back to his home. The animal Jamie had ridden in on was old, underfed and not capable of making the trip back on this night. The Hollisters could return the rented horse and pick up their own horse on their next trip into town.

Of course, the Hollisters had a poor reputation. Even Enoch, who was usually very generous about such matters, had long ago stopped giving that family credit. Sylvia was certain the pastor had made an arrangement with the livery owner, promising to make good on any money he might lose by renting a horse to Jamie.

'Giles Hobart is a fine man of God. He's just the preacher I want to preside at my wedding.'

Sylvia placed a hand over her mouth and hastily looked around. She was alone . . . thank goodness! Enoch, Jenny and Goliath were in the back room where Enoch was finishing up on the renovations. That back room was the topic that had led to her silly, carefree mood.

Less than an hour ago Enoch had said to her:

'I'll be doing some work in the back for a while. I'll take the girl and the dog with me. Shout if you need help.'

'You have sure put a lot of work into that back room.' She gave him a playful smile. 'First you built that big shed behind the store, and moved all the tools and such out there. Now, you're cleaning and painting the room. What exactly do you have in mind?'

Enoch immediately picked up on the playful mood. 'I've got a few notions which I just might someday let you in on. Meanwhile, I've showed you I'm more than just a counter-jumper.'

Those words stunned Sylvia. 'I never thought of you as a counter-jumper. And besides, I just work here; what difference does it make what I think?'

'You know I don't think of you as someone who just works here, you're the woman who I plan. . . .' Enoch lowered his head. When he looked up his eyes went directly to the little girl. 'Come with me, child, bring Goliath with you.' He couldn't look at Sylvia again as he hastily disappeared with Jenny and Goliath in tow.

Sylvia opened the accounts book but didn't look down at it. Enoch Brighton hadn't exactly proposed marriage to her, but surely he had made his intentions clear. Now it would only be a matter of time before. . . .

The young woman's musings were shattered by a piercing

scream. Jenny came running in from the back room.

'Goliath gone! Goliath gone!'

Sylvia couldn't immediately shake the cloud her thoughts were in. She placed a hand on Jenny's shoulders.

'Oh, I'm sure Goliath has just run out the back door chasing a rabbit or something. He'll be back—'

'No! Goliath gone!'

'Did you ask your Uncle Enoch about—'

'Gone!' the child screamed.

Sylvia's cloud dissipated. She wasn't sure if Jenny was now referring to Goliath or Enoch. She needed to find out for herself.

'Jenny, let's go find Goliath together.' The woman had tried not to let worry fracture her voice as she took the child by the hand.

Sylvia and Jenny ran through the store proper, through the door and into the mercantile's first storage room, which contained canned goods and other foodstuffs. The room was large and over-stocked. Sylvia and Jenny had to wind their way around stacks of crates containing canned beans and peaches before reaching that room's back door, which led to the room Enoch had been working on and which now stood almost empty.

Sylvia and Jenny stood in the dark room, the only light being provided by the sliver of milky white coming from the barely opened back door of the store.

'What happened to the lanterns Enoch keeps here for night work?' the woman asked out loud.

'Goliath, come!' Jenny shouted.

A scratching sound could be heard, followed by an anxious whine.

'There's a closet over here,' Sylvia pointed to her left and smiled at Jenny. 'Goliath must have wandered in and—'

A hand suddenly clamped over Sylvia's mouth. A hard object slammed against her wrist, forcing her to let go of

Jenny. An arm quickly moved cobra-like around her waist and she was pressed against her captor's body.

Sylvia watched in terror as a hooded figure grabbed Jenny and ran with her out the back door of the mercantile. She could hear horses whinny from nearby. The outlaws were grabbing Jenny and planned to ride off with her on horses tethered behind the store.

'Take things easy, girlie. I'm jus' gonna tie you up and let ya lie down peaceable like.'

Her captor's grip relaxed slightly. Sylvia took a small step forward and kicked the man's shin. He cursed loudly.

'If that's the way ya want it, girlie.' A sharp pain exploded in Sylvia's head and she dropped to the floor. Through hazy vision she watched her assailant run off through the back door. The escape of unconsciousness beckoned her but she refused to surrender.

'Help!' the woman shouted as she struggled to her feet and stumbled outside. Her vision was now clearing. She could see two hooded men running toward their horses, which were tied to a scraggly tree about fifteen feet away. One of the men carried Jenny.

Enoch came running at an unsteady gait from out of the shed. He was carrying a pistol. A rope dangled from one wrist.

'Let the child go,' he shouted.

The thug who was not carrying Jenny turned and fired at Enoch. The store owner replied with two red-orange flashes. The outlaw spun and dropped to the ground.

The second outlaw had placed Jenny on one of the horses and was preparing to mount. Enoch pointed his pistol at the hooded figure.

'Let the child go, *now*!'

The outlaw froze for a moment, making Enoch's order unnecessary. Jenny slid off the horse on the opposite side from her captor and ran toward Enoch.

The panicked thug mounted his horse. Enoch shouted a warning to stop as he prepared to fire again.

'What's going on?'

Startled, Enoch did a fast turn to face the newcomer standing beside him. The store owner heard the pound of hoofbeats from nearby. He quickly refastened his gaze on the thug who was now riding off, his body bent down on his horse's neck. The store owner's shot went over the outlaw, who spurred his roan around the saddle shop neighboring the mercantile.

'I'm sorry, Enoch,' Clint Mead loudly apologized. 'I thought I heard a scream for help, then I sure enough heard shots and came runnin'. Looks like I helped some coyote get away. I shoulda been more—'

'Jenny!' Sylvia embraced the child and lifted her into her arms. 'Everything is OK now, you're safe.'

'Goliath!' Jenny screamed.

'Goliath is just fine.' Sylvia hoped she was right. 'We'll go let him out of the closet.' She looked toward the men as she began to walk back to the store.

'The sheriff and I will be there in a moment.' Enoch pointed to the figure lying to the left of him. 'We gotta check on that owlhoot; it won't take long.' He mouthed the rest of his words: *Probably dead.*

Fifteen minutes later Sheriff Mead and the survivors of the attempt to kidnap Jenny were gathered in the back of Brighton's Mercantile. A lantern beamed light from where it stood on the floor. Sylvia was sitting on a stool she had brought in from the front of the store and was holding a wet cloth against the side of her head. Jenny stood beside Sylvia with one arm wrapped around Goliath, who had been found unharmed in the closet.

At Sylvia's insistence Enoch was also holding a wet cloth against a head injury but he had refused to sit down. Sheriff

Mead stood with his arms folded, looking angry with himself and the world in general.

'So, Sheriff, you recognized the outlaw Enoch killed?'

Sylvia's question did not appear to make him feel better.

'I spotted him in the Prairie Dog this afternoon. He claimed he'd jus' rode in. I tol' him he had ta have a job in one week, the usual stuff Bernard makes us say. . . . Guess the jasper don't have ta worry 'bout findin' a job no more.' The lawman unfolded his arms. 'Let's piece together what went on here tonight. Enoch, you go first.'

Now it was Enoch's turn to look angry with himself. 'I shouldn't have left Jenny alone, even for a moment.'

'Don't blame yourself, Enoch.' Sylvia spoke softly.

'Yep, don't blame yourself, Enoch.' Clint Mead's voice wasn't soft. 'Jus' tell us what happened.'

'Well, Jenny, Goliath and me were back here when I noticed an open crate half-full of hammers. This may surprise you, Clint, but we don't sell all that many hammers. I guess that's because a hammer can last almost forever. . . .'

'OK, I'm surprised; now get on with your story.'

'Sorry. I decided to take the crate of hammers out to the shed. Jus' when I was putting it in there I heard footsteps behind me, but too late. I got hit in the head really hard, must have been knocked out. When I came to I was lying on the floor with my arms tied behind me and a bandanna in my mouth. Of course, my gun was outta sight.'

'I guess ya couldn't have been tied up very good.'

'Whoever did it worked too fast,' Enoch agreed. 'It took time, of course, but I managed to get loose. Then I grabbed my gun. . . .'

'How'd you find your gun so quick in the dark?' Sylvia asked, her eyes remaining focused on Jenny.

Enoch gave the young woman a whimsical grin.

'The owlhoot that whacked me in the head grabbed my gun and tossed it into the dark. Before I passed out I heard

130

a certain clinking sound. My gun had landed in the crate of hammers.'

'Next time I'll be more polite when you start goin' on about hammers,' said the sheriff good-naturedly. 'Now, Miss Sylvia, could ya tell us what happened to you tonight?'

Sylvia provided a cautious, accurate description of everything that had happened to her and Jenny from the moment she heard the child screaming for help. But it was obvious that the young woman was more concerned about the immediate present. She caressed Jenny's head gently, afraid that the child was once again retreating into a cocoon of silence.

Her fear seemed justified. When Sylvia had finished with her account she whispered to Jenny:

'Those bad men are gone now, they won't bother you ever again.'

Jenny didn't respond. She continued to hug Goliath, her eyes filled with something distant and terrifying.

'Well ... I gotta look after that gent out back,' Clint mumbled. He left the premises by the back door.

As he made his way down Candler's main street Clint saw Rance Dehner and Boone Logan riding back into town. Both men looked worried as they pulled up their horses.

'Them Hollisters tricked us,' Boone shouted. 'Anything goin' on while we was gone?'

'Meet ya both at the office in a few minutes,' Clint replied. 'First, I gotta see the undertaker.'

Dehner and Logan exchanged hard glances. Their worst fears had been true.

CHAPTER TWENTY-FOUR

Several hours after listening to Clint Mead explain the attempted abduction of Jenny, Rance Dehner walked the streets of Candler, not really doing a complete round. His mind was too inwardly focused for that. He was recalling a conversation he'd had with his boss, Bertram Lowrie, on his first full day working for the Lowrie Detective Agency.

Lowrie, a retired British military officer, had come to America to start a ranch. For reasons that Lowrie never explained to Dehner, the ranch hadn't worked out. Lowrie had abandoned that dream and started a detective agency to compete with Pinkerton.

Bertram Lowrie was a tall man with iron-gray hair and a physique thin to the point of looking emaciated. Rance would learn, during the few cases on which they worked together, that his boss's frail appearance was very misleading.

But on this day, Bertram Lowrie had been primarily interested in quizzing his new employee.

'I know you worked a year for the Pinkertons, Mr Dehner.'

'Yes, sir.'

Both men were standing and Rance noted Lowrie's perfect posture and military bearing. The man had an ageless quality about him, which made guessing his age a futile endeavour.

'I can understand your leaving the Pinkertons,' Lowrie continued. 'Union busting is an ugly, unjust business. As for the domestic cases, peeking in windows at wayward husbands and all that. . . .'

Lowrie shook his head and rolled his eyes, indicating such lurid matters were beneath the dignity of gentlemen. 'But there is much good about the Pinkertons and your record indicates you benefitted from your association with them.'

Dehner sensed that Lowrie's last statement constituted a challenge.

His reply was crisp.

'Yes sir, my time with Pinkerton was most valuable.'

Lowrie's next words confirmed Dehner's suspicions:

'Please elaborate.'

'I learned the importance of gathering information and how you go about it. When I arrive in an area where there has been a crime or a series of crimes I stay there, observe and listen. Crime creates lies and lies become brittle and fall apart. I take in all the facts I can and try to piece them together. I never make an accusation I can't back up.'

Dehner stopped at a point slightly out of town and far beyond the boardwalk. He gave a stone a hard kick and watched it collide with a tree. Had he been too cautious with his investigation in Candler? Had he stuck with his own methods for too long? If he had moved sooner could lives have been saved?

The detective turned and walked toward his destination. He wasn't sure if he could back up his accusations, at least not to the point of justifying arrests. But he could wait no longer.

Rance opened the door of the First Church of Candler and walked inside. A few of the kerosene lamps in the sanctuary were lit, but only a few. This was not a public meeting.

Three men stood at the front of the church in front of the platform containing the pulpit and choir loft:: Giles Hobart, Doc Reggie and Boone Logan.

Hobart pulled out his pocket watch.

'One a.m. – you are right on time, Rance.'

'I want to thank you gentlemen,' said Dehner, 'for agreeing to meet me here and not telling anyone else about it. I know the request was a bit unusual but, you see, I need help and you three men are the only ones in Candler I can trust.'

'Sheriff Mead ain't here.' Boone looked confused. 'Don't ya trust him?'

'No, I make a habit of never trusting cold-blooded killers.'

CHAPTER TWENTY-FIVE

Dehner's three companions all looked shocked. Doc Reggie gave the customary response.

'You must be joking!'

Rance's reply was also the customary one: 'I wish I was.'

Reverend Hobart returned his pocket watch to its pocket. 'You have made a very serious allegation, Mr Dehner, please explain yourself.'

Despite the situation, Dehner was mildly amused by the formality of Hobart's statement, which reminded him of Bertram Lowrie. But the detective realized the stiffness was justified. His face remained solemn.

'As you gentlemen know, I originally came to Candler because I'm investigating a series of holdups and related killings which have been going on in this area. The gang that pulled these holdups usually consisted of four men.'

'Yeah,' Boone cut in. 'But ya tol' the sheriff and me ya thought there was only two men actually behind it. After they pulled the holdups, they'd kill the other two owlhoots and split the take between them. Candler is where they sorta hide out, passin' themselfs off as respectable citizens. Are ya sayin' Clint Mead is one of the outlaws?'

'Yes.' Dehner nodded his head. 'The other one is, or was,

Joshua Scott. Tillie Scott knew what was going on, but her participation was limited.'

Doc Reggie, the pastor, and the deputy were pacing about in the aisle between the pews, while Dehner stood still in the same area, his arms folded.

'Let's allow Rance to give us his . . . ah . . . theory,' the doctor suggested.

Dehner unfolded his arms and relaxed a bit. He was among skeptics, but skeptics who were willing to give him a chance.

'On the first day I met him Mead made some statements which seemed a bit strange. He told me he was supporting Enoch Brighton for mayor. A sheriff usually stays out of political races, except his own.'

'You're right,' Doc Reggie shrugged his shoulders,'but that hardly makes Clint a thief and a killer.'

'True,' Rance agreed. 'But he told me the town's current mayor, Bernard Candler, was preventing the railroad from coming into Candler. That's nonsense.'

'I don't follow you, Rance.' Giles Hobart's voice was no longer stiff and formal.

'That so-called railroad detective, Brad Cody, did make one true statement. Railroads are run by tough men who push hard to get what they want. They wouldn't be stopped by a small- town mayor. Oh, I'm sure they met with Bernard and tried to get him on their side. But the mayor's opposition meant very little; . . . he couldn't stop a railroad from buying up private property. No, Clint Mead had another reason for wanting Bernard Candler out as mayor.'

'And jus' what might that be?' Boone Logan asked.

'Bernard's demand that newcomers to town be questioned and given an ultimatum: find a job in one week or leave Candler.'

Doc Reggie's eyes became slits. 'I know what Bernard instructed is illegal . . . technically at least . . . but why should

Clint become so upset by such a small matter?'

'The sheriff and Joshua decided they couldn't continue with their holdups and killings much longer. Mead had purposely made life hard on his deputies so they wouldn't stay around long and get suspicious. But other folk were beginning to note Clint Mead's occasional absences. I rode with the sheriff out to the Brawley ranch to help with a problem there. Herb Brawley was so used to the sheriff being out of town, he had set up his own procedures for dealing with crooked ranch hands.'

The doctor still appeared unconvinced. 'Well, if Clint and Josh had decided to end their holdups . . . why would they worry about Bernard demanding that new arrivals explain themselves?

'Clint and Josh may have been finished with stagecoach and other holdups but they weren't through with crime. During their criminal activities they gained connections with a gang that was smuggling guns into Mexico.'

Boone waved a finger in Dehner's direction. 'Ya said something 'bout a US marshal goin' after a bunch that was gun smugglin'.'

'Mark Reno is the marshal's name,' Dehner said. 'He's a good lawman who made one serious mistake. He trusted Clint Mead. As a result, Mark's been riding a lot of trails to nowhere.'

The detective did a quick assessment of his companions. All three looked uncomfortable but for the right reasons. They didn't like what they were hearing but he was getting through to them.

Rance sighed, then moved into the toughest part of his narrative.

'Clint Mead wanted to get in on the gun-smuggling, but then Josh suddenly had a change of heart.'

'What kind of change?' Giles Hobart asked.

Dehner grinned at the pastor.

'We know Tillie Scott loved Jenny. I'm sure her husband shared that love. They wanted to give their child a good life and decided that having a father who was a thief and a killer could be a problem. Josh decided on honest work. He and Tillie were probably planning on really starting a horse ranch.'

'So, Clint Mead was left without a partner for the gun-smuggling operation,' Hobart speculated.

Dehner inhaled as if bracing for an assault.

'Clint found another partner: Enoch Brighton.'

Doc Reggie took a fast step backward and accidentally collided with a pew. 'Rance, I can't believe, I mean . . . Enoch has always been such an honest. . . .'

'You thought Clint Mead was honest, too.'

'If what you say about Enoch is true, Rance, this news will devastate Sylvia,' Giles Hobart declared.

Once again Dehner had to hide his amusement. Giles Hobart didn't sound terribly upset over Enoch Brighton no longer being a suitable husband for Miss Kaplan.

Deputy Logan brought the detective back to the immediate.

'You claim the railroad didn't care what Bernard thought, so how come they got all involved in the election for mayor?'

'They didn't.'

'What d'ya mean?' Logan demanded.

'Steven Montague was a total phony,' Dehner said. 'I sent a telegram to the Lowrie Agency and had them look into it. It didn't take long. There is no one named Montague working for the Union West Railroad.'

Boone's face became hard and intense. 'That means Brad Cody, the railroad detective, is also a phony!'

Dehner nodded his head. 'The guy who called himself Montague was just some jasper Brighton and Mead hired to make Enoch Brighton look good at that political rally. Mead probably arranged to meet him in a remote location to pay him off after the rally was over. The sheriff met him all right, and paid him off with lead.'

'I do remember the sheriff being gone for a while that night,' Boone affirmed. 'But wait a minute, Stephen Montague's brother came to town seeking vengeance for—'

Rance didn't allow the deputy to continue. He didn't want Boone to feel too foolish. 'Mead and his fellow crooks stumbled onto some good luck and all of us let him get away with it because of a very obvious mistake.'

'What's that?' Doc Reggie asked.

'Blond hair isn't all that common, so when we see two men with hair the colour of straw we have no problem believing they are related,' Rance explained.

'Ya mean that fella that got off the stage and caused all the trouble, he weren't really a crook?' Deputy Logan's face was ashen.

'I suspect he was an outlaw and was, as they say, touched in the head.' Dehner tried to sound comforting. 'The man was obviously dangerous and probably on the run, but when Mead and the jasper who calls himself Brad Cody found out a blond outlaw was lying in Doc Reggie's office, they had a new twist to their story of Steve Montague mysteriously disappearing. Cody snuck into the doctor's home and killed the gent, making us think Stephen Montague's brother had been murdered.'

'Who is this Brad Cody really?' Discouragement lay heavy in Boone's voice.

'I don't know his actual name,' Dehner admitted. 'But I'm sure he's a leader of the gang that is doing the gun-smuggling. He's here to help Enoch.'

Boone Logan's eyes looked down to the floor. Dehner realized what an outstanding lawman Boone would make some day. The deputy was devastated by his mistakes. He realized that when a lawman makes a serious blunder, the results could harm a lot of innocent people.

The detective spoke softly. 'Enoch had another round of good luck, and I'm afraid both you and I were part of it, Boone.'

Boone closed his eyes for a moment and nodded his head. 'Ya mean them two jaspers, Tom and Luke, the ones that tried to kill Enoch – or I thought they did.'

Dehner got to the point. 'Tom and Luke were two low level henchmen, working with the gun-smuggling outfit. They were sent here to look into some minor matters concerning the set-up with Enoch. You were right to follow those gents out of the Prairie Dog saloon to the back of Enoch's store. Enoch spotted you the moment you glanced through the back door. He had to convince you he was a victim of some kind or you would have wondered why he was doing business with two shifty characters.'

'But Luke and Tom. . . ? Those owlhoots were talkin' tough to Enoch . . .' Boone sounded confused, not defensive.

'Like a lot of thugs, they had an exaggerated idea of their own importance,' Dehner said. 'They were arguing about the set-up in the back of the store for hiding the guns. Remember, it was Enoch who instigated the fight.' The detective glanced around to take in all three men. 'Boone's vision was blocked by wooden crates. He couldn't see that Luke didn't have his gun out.'

The deputy threw his arms up. 'And when I got back to the store I declared that Enoch must have killed Luke while tryin' to wrestle the gun from him. I handed him a perfect story.'

'I was part of it too, Boone.' Rance spoke softly. 'I killed Tom when he tried to ride out of town.'

'I just can't believe Enoch is a crook.' Doc Reggie shook his head. 'Why, this evening Enoch rescued Jenny from—'

'That was a charade put on by Enoch Brighton and Sheriff Mead.'

The doctor's head shot back in surprise. 'Are you sure, Rance?'

'Yes. Enoch was preparing the back room of his store as a temporary hiding-place for the guns before they were moved south. But Bernard would get feisty over men coming and going in Candler without having an apparent reason to be here. So, Bernard Candler's reign as mayor had to come to an end. Both Enoch and Clint thought that would be easy, but it didn't turn out that way. The political debate backfired. The Bushrod brothers stole the show with their jokes and free candy. The election was tilting toward Bernard.'

'So tonight Enoch becomes a hero,' Doc Reggie said. 'He saves Jenny from being kidnapped and Sylvia serves as a perfect witness.'

'Exactly,' Rance affirmed. 'I'm convinced the jasper who calls himself Brad Cody is the man who grabbed the child. The other culprit was a low-level hood who was working with the gun smugglers. That jasper didn't know what was planned for him. Enoch killed the thug and made himself a hero in the process.'

Boone gave the detective a hard-edged smirk. 'Ol' man Ferguson, the circuit judge, gits real persnickety 'bout stuff like evidence. You got much in the way of proof?'

Dehner pressed his lips together, then replied:

'Tonight, someone locked Goliath in a closet before grabbing the kid. Goliath is very protective of Jenny. He would growl at any stranger who got near her. It took someone the dog trusted to lure him into a closet. That someone was Enoch Brighton.'

'And what 'bout Sheriff Clint Mead?' Boone persisted.

'Mead's behaviour at the political debate last Saturday was very strange,' Dehner reminded the three men. 'He blew up when he realized Enoch hadn't carried the day. He even tried to plant the notion that Bernard Candler had tried to have Enoch murdered, only to have that move fail, too.'

The deputy rolled his eyes. 'Your evidence is pretty weak; the judge ain't gonna be impressed.'

'And there are still a lot of unanswered questions, Rance,' Hobart said. 'Why were Tillie and Josh murdered and their house burned down, and why—'

Dehner held up his right palm in a stop gesture. 'There are a lot of questions in need of answers and I haven't got a shred of evidence to present in court. That's why I need help from you three.'

'What kinda help?' Boone asked.

'This case is coming to a head tomorrow and it is going to end where it began, with a little girl named Jenny.'

CHAPTER TWENTY-SIX

'Amen.'

Reverend Hobart lifted his head and smiled at the congregation in front of him. They weren't as well dressed as they would be on a Sunday morning but their faces were bright with anticipation. While the pastor would have liked to think the anticipation came solely from faith in the power of prayer, he knew better.

He closed the Bible on the pulpit in front of him.

'Unless there are some more prayer requests, I think we can bring this meeting to a close.'

Clint Mead stood up from the back pew. 'May I say a few words, Preacher?'

'Of course, Sheriff.'

Mead smiled at the gathering in front of him. 'As some of you folks may have noticed comin' in, there is a table set up jus' a short distance from the church. And as I had a chance to tell some of ya, Miss Sylvia Kaplan has been kind enough to prepare some cookies and lemonade for us.'

He paused and gave the children a mischievous grin. 'And I even unnerstand there jus' might be some candy for the kids. Ever'body is welcome!'

'Thank you, Sheriff Mead. And now, if there are no further—'

Rupert Bushrod stood up from the front pew. 'Preacher, may I say somethin'?'

'Yes, but please keep it brief, Brother Bushrod.' Giles's calling Rupert 'brother' was acceptable protocol in church. Besides, Rupert and Clarence had only begun attending services since the election started and Giles, who had made only one purchase at their store, had trouble telling them apart.

'I need to warn folks that this here is a violation of church and state.'

Giles cringed openly. He was already nervous enough. 'Please explain, Brother Bushrod.'

'Well, I suspect there's more to this here get together than jus' lemonade and treats. There's gonna be politikin' on behalf of Enoch Brighton. Mixin' politics and religion is wrong. Besides, those of us in the Bernard Candler camp didn't think of it ourselfs. We're sorta left with egg on our faces.'

'Never did quite git what havin' egg on your face meant, never had the problem myself,' Clarence Bushrod remained seated as he spoke, 'but then, I like my eggs scrambled. Maybe folks who like 'em sunny side up would—'

'Clarence, you sure have a way of bein' beside the point,' Rupert snapped at his brother.

The pastor's nervousness became more apparent.

'Gentlemen, please! I can assure—'

'May I speak for a moment, Reverend Hobart?'

'Yes, Mr Candler, of course.'

Bernard Candler stood up and smiled at the congregation as Rupert hastily sat down.

'We are blessed with a beautiful evening: a bright moon and a sky full of stars. There's even a cool breeze. We all know Sylvia Kaplan makes great lemonade and cookies. I will be at that table and happy to talk with anyone who wants to talk with me. But I promise, if Enoch Brighton makes a speech I will not demand to be granted a similar platform. At my age,

I need to preserve my energy.'

There was light, appreciative laughter. Reverend Hobart hastily dismissed the meeting.

'Looks like I proved to be a political genius once again,' Rupert whispered to his brother as they stood up to leave.

'If you ask me, Enoch Brighton is the one lookin' smart,' Clarence disagreed. 'No way this many folks will be in town agin before votin' day. We ain't got another chance to bribe 'em with free stuff.'

'Ya jus' don't understand, brother; in politiks ya gotta be quick on your feet and make the best of a bad deal. By speakin' up the way I did, I gave Bernard a chance to be a true gentleman. Ya gotta admit he sounded real good.' Rupert chuckled in a conspiratorial manner as the two men shuffled out of the church.

'Yep, he sure did,' Clarence admitted. 'Why, Bernard even smiled when he talked . . . downright threw some folks into shock.'

The two brothers were now outside the church. Rupert looked up to the stars. 'Let's hope the shock holds until votin' day.'

The crowd became increasingly giddy as they all made their way past the hitch rail in front of the church, wound their way around the buggies and buckboards, and mean-dered toward a large cottonwood. The tree stood alone in an otherwise vacant field and it was far enough away to counter Rupert's claims of threatening the divide between church and state. A table stood under the tree and, as promised, Sylvia Kaplan stood behind the table pouring lemonade into glasses. Four large plates of cookies adorned the table top.

The mood went from giddy to festive as people began to enjoy the treats and Enoch passed out pouches of candy to the children. Dehner watched the proceedings with an odd sense of terror. Most of the people gathered under the cot-tonwood were fine, hard-working folks who were enjoying a

145

moment of innocent fun. Yet there was a terrible evil behind all of this, an evil that had already reaped much bloodshed and from which much bloodshed could still come.

You're no philosopher, Dehner whispered to himself; *start thinking like a detective.*

A lantern hung on one of the branches of the distant cottonwood. Rance suspected it was there to provide a spotlight and he was right. About fifteen minutes into the fun, Clint Mead stood in the patch of kerosene-yellow glow and lifted his hands.

'Could I have your attention for jus' one moment – well, maybe two or three moments?'

The gathering responded with cheerful laughter and centered their attention on the sheriff, who continued in an amicable manner:

'As all of you know, I have been the sheriff of Candler for a long time.'

'You've been sheriff far too long, Clint,' Dehner shouted.

Uneasy laughter followed. Mead looked stunned but tried to maintain a happy mood.

'Rance can be a real joker sometimes—'

'I'm not joking, Mead.' Dehner checked Giles Hobart. The pastor had Jenny positioned where she had a good view of Clint Mead.

The detective stepped into the spotlight Mead had occupied alone. 'You murdered Tillie and Josh Scott, Clint Mead. You shot them down in cold blood.'

Shouts of anger and disbelief came from the crowd.

'Dehner here works for an outfit in Dallas.' Mead pointed at the detective. 'Guess he's like a lot of Texans, filled with hot air and wanting to push other people around.'

The crowd murmured in agreement. Dehner ignored them.

'Your game is up, you've fallen. You don't deserve to wear a star on your shirt, Clint Mead.' The detective grabbed Mead's

146

badge, ripped it from his shirt and tossed it to the ground.

'Starz falling! Starz falling!' Jenny shouted. The child ran toward Clint Mead, pointing a finger at him. 'You killed Mommy and Daddy.'

'That kid's loco!' Mead pushed Dehner aside and took a few quick steps toward the child.

A deep growl was followed by the roar of battle as a brown flash leaped toward the sheriff. Mead cried out in pain as Goliath sank his teeth into his leg. Mead tried to pull his gun but Dehner twisted the sheriff's arm, causing the gun to drop to the ground from where Giles Hobart scooped it up.

Clint Mead plunged to the ground. Goliath advanced onto the sheriff's chest. The dog's eyes focused on Mead's throat. Screams and shouts came from the crowd as people shifted about, not knowing what to do.

Doc Reggie knew what he had to do.

'Sit boy, sit.' He placed a hand on Goliath. The dog obeyed but kept fierce eyes on Mead and growled in a threatening manner.

'Mr Logan, are you all right?'

Dehner turned his head toward the female shout. Through the panicked scurrying of the crowd he could see Logan getting back on his feet.

'I'm fine,' the man was declaring angrily.

The detective shifted his glance between the doctor and the pastor.

'Can you gents handle Mead?'

'If we can't, Goliath will do the job for us,' Doc Reggie answered.

As Dehner scrambled toward the deputy he saw Sylvia Kaplan with her arms protectively around Jenny. This night would become an even worse nightmare for the young woman but Rance didn't have time to dwell on that.

He made his way through a circle of townspeople to where the deputy stood, gently running a hand under his right eye.

'What happened?' Dehner snapped the question.

'Brad Cody, the phony railroad detective, sucker-punched me. He and Enoch ran off toward the church – there's lots of horses there.'

Dehner didn't bother asking about Boone's health. The detective knew what the answer would be.

'Let's move,' he said. He turned to the people surrounding them. 'The rest of you stay here.'

'Careful, Dehner,' a man from the crowd shouted. 'Enoch's carrying a gun but that jasper he's after could be a gunfighter.'

As Rance and Boone broke away from the cottonwood and the people gathered under it, they could see two shadows running toward the church. Nearing the hitch rail, the shadows turned around and viewed their pursuers. One shadow motioned with his arm toward the church and both figures ran inside.

Dehner and Logan pounded their way to the church, then stepped lightly onto the porch and positioned themselves on each side of the open double doors; each man held a gun in his hand.

'Does the church have another door?' asked Dehner.

'There's a back door.' Like Dehner, the deputy spoke in a low whisper. 'Reckon they're still inside?'

Dehner thought about it for a moment, but only for a moment.

'The way I see it, both Cody and Brighton know their plans are finished. You got it right, they were headed for the horses.'

Logan cautiously peered inside the church. All he could see was darkness.

'Why didn't they jus' ride off?'

'We were too close, there'd have been a good chance we could shoot them out of their saddles.'

Boone grimaced. 'Most folks back there got no idea what's

goin' on, 'cept Doc Reggie and the preacher.'

'And those two are busy with Clint Mead,' Dehner said.

'Enoch and Cody must figger if they get rid of us they can ride off, free as birds.'

Dehner nodded his head. 'Stay here and watch the front. I'll check the back. They may be hiding in the woods behind the church.'

Dehner stepped off the porch and cautiously made his way to the back of the small building. No one was there but the detective wasn't really expecting anyone. The patch of sparse grass buffering the church from the woods provided no help. July was a hot, dry season: there were no footprints.

Holding his .45, Dehner listened closely as he looked toward the woods. He figured his prey wouldn't move too far away. Their goal was to get back to the front of the church and the horses. Of course, they could still be inside the church planning an escape through the front door. For a man who had only been a deputy for a short time Boone Logan was getting plenty of experience.

A light wind rattled the leaves. To his left Dehner thought he heard branches making more noise than could possibly be stirred by the breeze. Someone was climbing a tree. The detective slowly entered the forested area.

As he moved forward Dehner noted the trees were huge and far apart but became thinner and closer together as you went further into the woods. Cody and Brighton couldn't help but make a lot of noise if they ran into all that foliage. The outlaws had to be nearby.

From the corner of his eye Dehner spotted movement behind a large tree a few feet in front of him. He holstered his weapon and dropped his gaze, pretending to be studying the ground. He moved past the tree, then turned and grabbed the arm of Brad Cody, who was about to assault Dehner's head with the butt of a pistol.

The gun fired into the ground before Dehner could force

the phony railroad detective to drop it. Cody broke loose from Dehner and tried to pick up the gun. Dehner kicked him below the knee, sending the outlaw sprawling onto his face.

Rance grabbed Cody's gun as he heard footsteps running toward him. Boone Logan appeared, weapon in hand; he looked on as Cody, trying to get back onto his feet, collapsed in the effort.

'Where's Brighton?' the deputy asked.

A shaking of branches above answered the question.

'Look out!' Dehner yelled.

A red-yellow flame came from the tree where Cody had been hiding. The flash briefly illuminated the panicked expression on Enoch Brighton's face as he lost his balance and plunged to the ground.

A bullet whined harmlessly into the air as Enoch landed face down with a thump. The storekeeper bellowed an angry string of obscenities, while Dehner ran toward him and yanked the gun from his right hand.

'I think my arm is broken.' Brighton screeched with pain as he turned over onto his back.

Rance looked at Boone Logan, who was standing over Brad Cody with his gun at the ready. Dehner then crouched beside the storekeeper and examined his injured arm, or pretended to.

'Yep, it's broken. We'll get you to Doc Reggie. He'll get you patched up in time to be hanged for killing Josh and Tillie Scott.'

'Is that what Mead told ya?' Brighton's voice was still a screech.

'Sure is.' Dehner smiled and nodded his head as he spoke the falsehood.

'Mead's a damn liar! Josh Scott and Mead were pards in a bunch of holdups—'

'When did you figure out they were pulling the holdups?' Dehner asked.

'A year or so ago; a storekeeper can learn a lot by keepin' his eyes open.' Brighton's voice calmed as it took on a boastful nature. 'Tillie Scott would come alone to the store at the same time Mead was gone. When the newspapers came in I read the stories about the holdups and realized they always happened when Mead and Scott were gone.'

Dehner maintained a calm façade. Enoch Brighton was a thief and a killer, but a smart one whose plans had almost succeeded. Brighton knew he was facing a rope and, like so many of his kind, would want to do some bragging to impress the people who would be watching him hang.

'You wanted in on the action, didn't you, Enoch?' Rance's voice was casual and friendly.

'Didn't care to spend my whole life standin' behind a counter, so I had a talk with Clint Mead.'

'How did the sheriff respond to you wanting to join the club?'

'He was right pleased. Tol' me he and Josh had only a few more robberies planned. They was gettin' involved with a gang smugglin' guns and Brighton's mercantile could be a great place to hide the guns before takin' 'em into Mexico.'

'Why did you kill Josh and Tillie Scott?' Dehner moved into the harder questions.

'That was Mead. Josh and Tillie got religion, wanted to walk the straight and narrow. Clint didn't think we could trust 'em. They knew too much and sooner or later, they jus' might blabber. So, Mead went out to their place, makin' it look like a social call.'

'He killed Josh and Tillie, but Jenny got away.'

Enoch gently touched his injured arm. 'When are ya gettin' the doc?'

'Soon enough.' Dehner's reply was crisp. 'Tell me about Jenny.'

'Ya got it right. Jenny ran and Clint couldn't find her till he spotted her with you. He tried to kill both of ya but couldn't do it. Rode back to town and tol' me what happened. And then you showed up with the girl.'

Rance could hear cautious footsteps; from the corner of his eye he saw people drawing near. Some curious folks had grown tired of waiting under the cottonwood tree.

'When did Mead realize his badge was still back at the Scott ranch?'

'He tol' me 'bout it soon as he got back to town. Tillie ripped the tin off his shirt before he killed her. He forgot 'bout it while runnin' after the kid. At first he didn't worry none. There were extra badges in his desk and he could go back and get the one he lost later on.

'But in the store I asked if I could ride with him out to the Scott place. He knew turning me down would make him look suspicious.

'When Sylvia asked if she could take Jenny home, Mead gave me a hard look. He needed me to help him. We came up with a plan, quick like. While he stalled you I rode out and when I couldn't find the damn badge I burned the place down. I took a few shots in your direction when ya got close to the ranch. That would stop ya from connectin' the killin's to Clint Mead.'

Dehner realized Tillie Scott had caused the downfall of a killer by ripping Mead's badge off his shirt. Giles Hobart had told him someone had returned to the Scott ranch the night he was in the underground hideout. The detective had eventually connected that someone with Clint Mead's fresh shirt and shiny badge when he first met him. Jenny's scream when she was hypnotized, about 'starz falling', led him further in that direction.

The detective looked away from Enoch Brighton and spotted a strange assembly of people standing several feet away. A group of townsfolk were huddled together near where Boone Logan had the phony railroad detective under guard. Most of the people looked oddly frozen, as if they were in a photograph. At the center stood Sylvia Kaplan, her face pale, with stony eyes. She had one arm around Jenny. The young woman seemed to be getting some sense of desperately needed support from the child. Jenny's face reflected a knowledge no child should have. The girl's arm rested on Goliath. The dog looked troubled. He knew something was very wrong but didn't know what to do about it.

Rance Dehner felt the same way.

CHAPTER TWENTY-SEVEN

The night was far from over. Using a method he had learned from Bertram Lowrie, Dehner kept the three outlaws separated. Enoch Brighton was taken to Doc Reggie's house. After his leg had been bandaged Clint Mead was led to a jail cell. The man who called himself Brad Cody was kept in the sheriff's office under the watchful eyes of both Boone Logan and Giles Hobart.

As Doc Reggie attended to his patient's broken arm Enoch babbled furiously to Dehner. He angrily denounced the 'morons' he had been working with. In the process he did spew out more information.

'That damned fool who helped out with the phony kidnappin' last night . . . like we tol' him, he fired wide so as not to hit me. Bet he was some surprised when I shot him down dead.'

'Who concocted the scheme involving the Hollisters?'

'Mead. But it was Cody who put on a hood and made the deal with Levi.'

'Did you plan on marrying Sylvia?' Dehner asked.

'Yep. One look at her and ya know why. The woman woulda' never figgered out what the back room was really bein' used for.'

154

Rance doubted that but saw no reason to pursue it. Instead the detective asked a question to which he almost didn't want to hear the answer:

'What plans did you have for Jenny?'

'I needed to kill her.' Brighton smirked in an offhand manner as if the question were not really important. 'Sooner or later she woulda got better and tol' ever'one Clint Mead murdered her people.'

'You reprehensible snake!' Doc Reggie could keep silent no longer. 'Pretending to care for that child. You knew what hell she was going through, seeing the man she'd watched kill her parents being treated like a respected citizen. That was probably one of the things keeping her locked up inside.'

Brighton's smile turned into a mocking laugh. Doc Reggie's arm raised as his hand became a fist. Rance grabbed the doctor's wrist.

'Hold off, Doc, you really don't want to do that.'

'Yes I do. This man's a monster. He doesn't deserve to live.'

'He's not going to,' Dehner said confidently.

Boone Logan's questioning of Brad Cody also produced valuable information. Cody admitted to heading up a gun-smuggling operation. He had sent Luke and Tom to Candler in order to learn how Enoch was coming along with the back room. But Enoch had later told Cody that Luke began to argue with him and when Boone came along Brighton decided to make it look like an attempt on his life.

Cody had also provided the man who claimed to be Stephen Montague.

'That jasper fancied himself a great outlaw. He wasn't much, could barely handle a gun. But he talked better than most. So I sent him to Candler to pretend he was some high-falutin muckety-muck from the railroad. Mead and I kept in

155

touch through the telegraph. We had ourselves a right fancy code no one else could make out.'

Giles Hobart, who was a witness to the interrogation, asked a question of his own.

'What about the blond-haired man you murdered?'

Cody didn't deny the accusation in the pastor's question.

'Got no idea who that fool was but, with the blond hair and all, he sure helped us build our story. Hell, we even planted some notions 'bout people gettin' killed because of the railroad. Hoped to get folks thinkin' Bernard Candler was behind it all – and it almost worked. Yep, never saw that blond jasper before. He was just a stroke of good luck.'

Boone gave the phony detective a genuine smile.

'Well, your good luck has jus' run out.'

Sunup was about three hours away when Brighton, Cody, and Clint Mead were placed in jail cells. The sheriff's office contained only three cells. Mead had to share a cell with Jake, the horse thief he had brought in only two days before.

Both Rance and Boone dozed for a couple of hours in the sheriff's office, Boone on a cot and Rance in a chair. Both men were up and discussing who would go to the café to get breakfast for the prisoners when Bernard Candler entered the office.

'Good morning, gentlemen; I'm sorry to bother you so early.'

'G-good morning. . . . 'Boone stuttered, 'ah . . . Your Honour.'

Bernard moved to the point. 'Reverend Hobart has just informed me of everything that happened last night. I still can't believe it, but I want to thank both of you gentlemen for what you have done for this town.'

Dehner and Logan both nodded politely.

The mayor continued: 'Boone Logan, I am here to officially appoint you acting sheriff. You will hold the office for

156

six months at which time you will have to run for office.'

'Thanks . . . ah. . . .'

'The circuit judge will arrive on Monday. Meanwhile this town will be experiencing a lot of high-strung emotions.' The mayor shifted his eyes to Rance. 'Mr Dehner, I would be most appreciative if you could remain in Candler for another week or so. I'm sure we can find some resources in the town's treasury to pay you.'

'I appreciate the offer, Mr Candler. I'll stay but I prefer to remain a volunteer.'

'Thank you, sir.' The mayor paused as if he needed to say something else. Unable to think of what it was he settled for: 'We all have a lot to do. I will be seeing you gentlemen later.'

As he started out the door Boone shouted out:'Good luck with the election, Mr Candler!'

The banker paused in the open doorway and a silly grin creased his face.

'I really don't think I'll be requiring much in the way of luck. My only opponent is in jail charged with murder. I'd say my chances of winning are rather good.' He barked a loud laugh as he closed the door behind him.

Bernard had been right. Candler became a town in turmoil with the former sheriff and one of its most trusted citizens in jail. But by Monday the mood had turned almost festive. Brad Cody had been turned over to US Marshal Mark Reno the previous day. Cody was already wanted for several murders connected to the gunrunning. But Candler still had two killers and a horse thief for the circuit judge to try. To the surprise of no one, all three were found guilty and sentenced to hang.

The construction of a gallows delayed the hangings until Wednesday. After the demands of justice were carried out the town's bars and eating-places did a robust business.

The Wednesday-night prayer meeting was also well attended. Following the meeting, folks departed appearing satisfied but exhausted by all that had happened.

Outside the church Bernard Candler motioned to several people to gather around him. Dehner was one of those folks, along with Boone Logan, Giles Hobart, Doc Reggie and Sylvia, who had Jenny with her. Jenny was, as always, accompanied by Goliath.

'I'll keep this meeting short.' The mayor spoke in a low voice as most people were riding off. 'But there are some changes coming up and I'll need your help.'

'Sylvia,' Bernard looked directly at the young woman, 'the bank is taking over Brighton's mercantile. I want you to change the name of the store and become the manager.'

Sylvia Kaplan's face remained pale and stoic. It had been that way since she learned the truth about Enoch Brighton.

'B-but sir . . .' the woman stammered as she looked down at Jenny.

'I know, your first commitment is to the child,' Bernard said approvingly. 'That's why I will be providing you with two helpers . . . the Bushrod brothers.'

'Wha—?' The stunned response came from everyone.

'Both Reverend Hobart and I have talked with the brothers and believe they are capable of . . . ah . . . becoming more responsible,' the mayor explained.

'I can second what Mr Candler just said, Miss Kaplan,' Giles spoke softly. 'Please be assured I will be keeping an eye on Rupert and Clarence.'

For the first time in a week Sylvia Kaplan gave a genuine smile. 'W-e-l-l, they will make me laugh and I haven't been doing much of that lately.'

Giles Hobart again spoke softly as he said some reassuring words. Dehner had noticed that the pastor had been attentive to Sylvia over the last week, but not pushy. Giles would make his feelings known when the time was right.

'Sheriff Logan,' Bernard continued, 'you will—'

'Excuse me, folks,' Dehner cut in, 'but I need to be

moving on.'

'Ya mean you're leavin'?' Boone asked.

What followed was a confusion of babble as people told Dehner he should wait until morning to ride out, and perhaps even give some thought to settling in Candler. The detective politely rebuffed all such remarks.

He untied his bay from the rail in front of the church. He already had all his belongings in the saddlebags. Dehner shouted one more polite 'goodbye' to the group as he rode off.

Rance stopped his horse when they had gone a fair distance and looked back. The small circle of people was still there, intently discussing their future and the future of a town that was only beginning to recover from a horrible shock. The detective's eyes settled for a moment on Jenny. The child had several people and a dog who loved her. Rance felt good about her chances of recovery.

Dehner knew the real reason he was leaving; it was that feeling he had at the conclusion of every case: a feeling that he no longer belonged. He wished the very best for the people of Candler but knew he could no longer be one of them.

Though they were not looking his way Rance gave the small group of people he still regarded as friends a final two-fingered salute. He then turned his horse and vanished into the night.